INMATE

*Write your stories.
Write the stories
of others. Always*

[signature]

CHRISTINE HALVORSON

Harmon House
Copyright © 2018 Christine Halvorson
All rights reserved.
ISBN-13: 978-0990939467

DEDICATION

This book is dedicated to my grandmother, Ethelyn Gertrude Thompson, whose true story we will never know, and to immigrant and poor girls who never got a chance to have grandchildren of their own who would attempt to tell their stories.

CHAPTER 1

We didn't have any bread in the house for breakfast, so while we waited I walked little Violet around the front room. That's when Papa stumbled in our front door, clutching his throat and mumbling something in Norwegian before he fell to the floor.

"Mama!" I screamed toward the kitchen. "Pearl!"

They came running and I dumped Violet in her cradle. We pulled and yanked at Papa's arms to get him up, but we weren't getting anywhere. Pearl was finally able to grab him around the waist and hoist, while Mama and I got him sort of balanced. I'd never seen anyone the color Papa was now. His face was brown and purple like a big bruise, like if you'd taken a colored man and smudged ink on him.

"Hjelpe mei! Hjelpe mei!" Papa screamed as Mama and Pearl lugged him to the bedroom at the back.

He couldn't be drunk. Not this early. Norwegian came out of him only when he was drunk, I knew that. It was forbidden for any of us to speak it; that was Papa's own rule. I knew something terrible was happening, Papa home in the middle of the morning. Home before eight when he'd only left at six, and screaming Norwegian?

I snatched up Violet and by the time I got to the back bedroom, Mama and Pearl had managed to get Papa on the bed. He was shivering so and his arms flailed at Pearl's face.

"Papa stop! Stop it," Pearl hollered, trying to hold his hands.

Mama wasn't strong enough to hold him down either. Violet started her own screaming and I bounced her on my hip as I watched and tried to shush her at the same time. Mama and Pearl finally got the sheets and blankets over him, then Mama quick pushed the window up, letting in a cold fall breeze. She dragged the corner chair over to the bed and plopped herself in it, yanking the braid loose from the top of her head.

"Nei, Thomas," she said to Papa, shaking her head to loosen her hair. "Nei. I will not have this. I won't, you hear, Thomas? Nei, nei, nei."

No, no, no. Was Mama trying to talk Papa out of being sick? She looked more angry than I've ever seen her. It was like she was shaking her finger at Papa for breaking something or talking back, like she'd done with me hundreds of times.

Pearl moved a cloth over Papa's forehead with one hand while she tried to keep the blanket on him with the other. He shivered and shook. It looked to me like he was getting even more purple. Mama just kept her eyes locked onto Papa's, which weren't even open any more. I wanted to watch what was going on, but Violet continued to wail in my ear. I sat with her on the floor over in the corner and pushed a wooden block toward her to keep her busy. Violet laughed, her face still soaked with crying. Was Papa going to die like so many others in the neighborhood? I'd heard the stories all week, but my Papa was strong as a horse.

We never saw Papa during the day. Ever. He wasn't very often home at night unless it was to stop in to eat a cold meat sandwich and drink a cup of coffee after his work day. He might wash his hands and face before going down to the corner bar to meet the other men of the neighborhood to argue in Norwegian about politics or complain about their jobs. He went out every night whether Mama was mad or not.

Pearl was now acting like she was the kindly nurse with Papa, instead of the nagging boss she was the rest of us all the time.

"Come on now, Papa. Keep the blanket on. Let me wipe your head," she murmured as she moved over him. "There now, isn't that better?"

Papa still fought her. Pearl straightened up and yelled. "Where is Berneeta, for heaven's sakes?"

She tried again to hold Papa's wrist over his head as he pushed at the washcloth. Mama had sent Berneeta out for our morning bread, to Josie's store where she got it for free since she worked there. "Gerty, you're going to have to go look for her."

"No, I'm not," I said right back. "I'm watching Violet and staying here."

Pearl liked being the boss of all of us, since she was 22 already, and right now I guess she had to be. Mama just leaned on the bed by Papa's face, and she rocked back and forth in the heavy old chair that didn't rock.

"Mama, is Papa going to die?" I asked.

She didn't answer so I pushed another block across the floor to Violet. Violet gave a happy squeal. "Mama?" I said again.

Mama didn't even look at me, but I knew I wasn't the only one in the room thinking Papa was going to die. Two more men in the neighborhood had died on Monday.

"Hush now. Don't we have enough trouble without your pestering?" Pearl hissed at me. She went back to wiping Papa's forehead.

Pearl's top braid had not even been done that morning. Everyone in the room looked pretty ragged.

My two braids weren't in yet either, but I was determined not to have it braided for school anyway. Braids were so babyish and old-fashioned. I wanted a short bob like some of the other ninth grade girls were wearing, or the working girls I saw on the streetcars. Mama wouldn't let me have a bob. She said it wasn't respectable for a young lady.

Bernie slammed the bedroom door open. "What are you all doing in here? The bread..."

She stopped when she noticed Papa in the bed. "What's going on? I've got bread."

"Berneeta," Mama said without looking up and Papa started moaning again. "Go back to the store right now and ask Josie if she knows where the doctor is."

"Pearl should go. What's going on? I want to stay with Papa," Berneeta whined and moved toward the bed.

"Berneeta, I said go!" Mama barked at her as she brushed her long hair out of her face, now wet from her own sweat.

"Oh, criminy," Berneeta said, but she stomped back out.

Pearl gave me her cloth and said I should go rinse it at the pump out at the side yard. "Get it good and cold. Take Violet with you. I can't stand her squealing another minute."

I knew it wasn't the time to argue with Pearl or to make Mama more mad. I grabbed Violet from the floor and went without saying a word, thinking how Berneeta really did whine too much for somebody who was 20 years old and helping the family with her job. Sometimes her food from the store is what kept us from starving, when Papa drank up his paycheck and Pearl's handwork didn't come through for the week. The war and, before that, moving to Minneapolis hadn't helped us one bit around here.

I set Violet in the dried up leaves by the pump and saw that Mrs. Jordahl, our landlady, was cleaning stems and weeds out of her kitchen garden up against the house.

"How's your papa, dear?" she called over to me.

"Purple and moaning," I told her.

Just then Papa screamed plain as day, again in Norwegian. We could hear him through the bedroom window that Mama had opened to let out the germs.

"Gott. Gott, hjelpe mei!"

I think he said he needed God's help. My Norwegian wasn't so good anymore. Mrs. Jordahl came over to pat Violet's head. Then she touched my hand as she moved toward the back door that led upstairs to her apartment.

"You come up and see me if you need to," she said. "I just baked cookies."

"Ja, tak," I said. I couldn't remember the last time I had eaten a cookie.

I snatched Violet up and rushed back into Papa's room with the wet cloth. He screamed and screamed, but he seemed asleep at the same time. He twisted left and right.

Mama and Pearl were holding him down again, Mama's long hair getting in the way. Papa's mouth gurgled with blood and he seemed to be choking now, the screams had stopped. Pearl pushed my hand away when I offered the cloth.

"Get away!" she snapped. "Play with Violet."

This time I was happy not to be watching Papa. I sat and pushed another block at Violet, put the cloth on my head and made a face at her. Anything to keep us busy. Violet laughed again, but my stomach felt kind of sick. Another block. Another squeal from Violet.

"Stop it now, you two. Quiet!" Mama stood up at the bed.

There wasn't any sound coming from Papa.

I couldn't hear gurgling or moans. No screaming. No Norwegian.

I couldn't look. I put Violet on my lap and leaned my chin on her head. Berneeta came through the door.

"Josie says the doctor's too busy. Everybody in the neighborhood is sick, she says. All the men anyway."

But Mama didn't look at Berneeta. Neither did Pearl. I set Violet back on the floor and stood up to see Papa was turning a different color now, a white-white on his forehead and a kind of blue on his arms. His chin was red. There was blood on the mess of sheets and blanket.

"Mama, did you hear me?" Berneeta whined. "Mama?"

"He's gone now. Gone."

Gone? I stepped over to pick up one of Papa's hands. It flopped in the air.

"Mama?" I tried to look at Mama. She kept her eyes on Papa.

"Gerty, it'll be alright."

Mama plopped back in her chair and cried.

Mama never cried.

CHAPTER 2

I thought I would go on just standing in that bedroom when Papa died because where else would I go? What else mattered now? I didn't know what people did when somebody died. For once, I wanted Pearl to tell me what to do. None of us moved. Nobody was crying. Nobody was talking. The four of us just stood around that bed and let little Violet play with blocks on her own. We would probably be standing there today if the doctor hadn't come--I don't know how many minutes, hours later--and Mama told us all then to go out to the kitchen and wait.

I don't remember much about what happened after that. I know Mrs. Jordahl brought us cookies. Those might have been the first cookies we had had since the war started four years ago. That's what I remember of that day Papa died. Warm cookies and thinking about the war.

Pearl really was the boss then because the next day Mama got sick, too. Oh, she didn't collapse like Papa had. She didn't scream in Norwegian. She just laid down on that same bed with her breathing sounding like water struggling to go down the clogged drain at the pump outside. I hadn't heard of any ladies dying of the Spanish Flu, but what could we do now?

Pearl took care of Mama and said I was in charge of Violet. Berneeta got us food from Josie's store, and somebody in the neighborhood had knocked on the door and gone away, leaving a basket of cheese and sausage.

Sure, Mama had said it was all going to be alright, but I didn't really see how. She went to bed, Papa was gone, and we four girls, if you count Violet, were left to figure things out. On the second morning after he died, I woke up with a thought in my head, or maybe it was a dream that woke me. I went to tell Pearl.

"We're supposed to have a funeral," I said when I found her and Berneeta in our tiny kitchen. "Shouldn't we call the pastor or something?"

"We can't afford a funeral and, besides, the paper yesterday said no one in Minneapolis can have one. They're banned, so just stop talking about it, Gerty," Pearl said.

"I will if you stop calling me Gerty," I said to her for the millionth time in my life. Gertrude was my middle name. Gerty--which Pearl and Bernie had called me since I was three--sounded like a cow's name, I thought, and I just knew my real name, Ethelyn, sounded like singing, though nobody could ever spell it correctly.

"It's not fair," Bernie said as she spread lard on her bread. "Papa should be buried in Albert Lea with the rest of the family, shouldn't he? Down where we left Sadie?"

"And how are we supposed to pay for that?" Pearl snapped, rinsing out Mama's breakfast dishes in a pan on the stove. "Do you think we can all just hop on a train for free and go to Albert Lea, lugging Papa with us? Think for once, Bernie," Pearl said, stopping her dishwashing long enough to poke her finger into Bernie's forehead.

"So, where did they put Papa?" I asked with a mouth full of bread. I was wondering if it was the cemetery I saw from the streetcar every day on my way to school.

"How am I supposed to know?" Pearl answered.

12

"You always act like you know everything," I said, sticking my tongue out at her. "I'm going to ask my teacher today. She'll know."

"You can't go to school today, Gertie," Pearl said. "People will talk."

"Talk about what? What do you mean?" I asked. "It's Monday. I should go to school."

"It's not proper. We're in mourning." Pearl said, as if this explained it well enough. "You can go tomorrow, but not today."

I didn't see what difference it made. Who was going to know my Papa died to even say anything? I loved school. I was the smartest in ninth grade and Mrs. Landry often told me she wished she didn't have to spend so much time with the others. She could pay more attention to me, she said, if the others were as good in English as I was. I didn't mind, though. I was just as happy to read books while she worked with the others.

Today my job, again, was to keep Violet from toddling off the porch steps or bothering Mama. I walked with Violet--front room, kitchen, Mama's room, the bedroom us girls shared--and back again. The only time Violet didn't fuss was when she sat on my hip, so we walked and I thought. I thought about what we were going to do with Papa gone and Mama sick. One thought I had, and maybe this was wrong of me, was that maybe things were going to be better because Papa wouldn't be around to drink up Pearl's pay or eat the little bit of food Bernie brought us from the store. Maybe Mama would get happy again, once she got well, of course.

The next day I left Violet in Pearl's care, Bernie went to work at the store, and I got on the streetcar for school.

Nobody asked me anything and my friend, Kjersti, whose father had died before Papa, wasn't even there. She would have been the only one I would tell anyway. And my teacher. It seemed like maybe something she'd like to know.

After school I asked Pearl, "Is Bernie's food and your sewing going to be enough for us?"

"Oh, be quiet, Gerty," Pearl had said. "We can't worry about that now."

I thought it was a good question. Who was going to make the money now?

Mrs. Landry told me today that Papa had probably been taken to Ashby Hospital, which would have seen about his burial. She said the same thing Pearl had said-- no funerals allowed in Minneapolis. She also said nobody in the city was allowed to go to church now because everybody might get sick. "No events where there might be crowds," Mrs. Landry explained. I didn't think a funeral for Papa would get a crowd, but I didn't say that to Mrs. Landry. "We were almost done with dying in the war and now this disease," she said. "I'm sorry for your loss, Ethelyn."

Mrs. Jordahl brought us a little food in that first week and today I found her sitting with Pearl at our wobbly table in the kitchen. Pearl was looking through Mama's box of old letters, the one Mama kept in her bureau drawer and I snuck in and read sometimes.

"Aunt Hattie?" Pearl was saying, handing an envelope to Mrs. Jordahl. "She lives down in Albert Lea, where Papa worked in that boarding house. Her only son's off to the war."

14

"Ja, ottern? Any others?" Mrs. Jordahl asked, but then she noticed me standing in the doorway. "Hello dear. Are you home?"

Of course I was home. What a dumb thing to say.

"What are you doing?" I asked Pearl.

Pearl ignored me and just kept waving the letters one by one at Mrs. Jordahl.

"Uncle Bernie? That's who Berneeta is named after," Pearl said. "He's Papa's brother. I think we heard he got hurt in the war, though. He's in Iowa. Aunt Sigrid, Mama's other sister, is up in Brooten? She and her husband run a logging camp."

Mrs. Jordahl stood up. "Ja, we write to them all," she said and took the three letters in their envelopes, giving me a pat on the hand as she left.

"Why is Mrs. Jordahl going to write our aunts and uncle when we never do?" I asked Pearl. I never even saw Uncle Bernie in my life and Aunt Sigrid just the once at the train depot for five minutes. I thought Mrs. Jordahl was maybe going to help us tell them Papa died and Mama was sick because she could write Norwegian.

"Gerty, I can't take care of us all. What's Mama gonna do? Get a job with Violet and you underfoot? Mrs. Jordahl's writing to ask family for help," Pearl said. "What she's really worried about is getting her rent money. She's not just being nice."

That night I could hear Pearl and Bernie whispering in their big bed, me and Violet on the other side of the room. They always thought I was asleep when I wasn't and I got to learn lots of things this way and hear a lot of things I wasn't supposed to hear.

15

"Aunt Hattie will probably take Mama. We can go up to Brooten. I know Aunt Sigrid will let us board with her if we do work," Pearl was saying. "She told Mama in one of those letters that logging was always busy and she even suggested we all come up there. Of course, that was two years ago now."

"What about Gerty?" Bernie asked.

"I think she should finish school or something. One of us should. She's too young to be on her own."

Too young to be on my own?! That made me mad, but what was I going to do, throw something at her?

"She is not too young." Bernie was whining again. "She's fifteen. I've been working since I was fifteen. Mama was married when she was fifteen."

"Gerty's sure not getting married. None of us are with all the boys gone or dead. Look at us already, me an old maid and you twenty!"

I was thinking nobody's going to marry Pearl anyway. Who would want her? Bernie had the good looks in the family and when she had money, she was always dolling herself up. Pearl and Bernie kept whispering, but I was getting so sleepy I was having trouble following what they were saying. How was I supposed to stay here in school? Living with what family? I'm going to make my own plans. They're not going to boss me around this time.

CHAPTER 3

About two weeks after Papa died, Mama said she felt a little better and got herself out of bed every now and then. She couldn't carry Violet though, and right away I noticed Mama's stomach was a little bigger, especially for a person who had not eaten very much in two weeks.

A baby? Oh, no. We just got Violet to try walking a little and we didn't need another baby. Mama was getting too old. There had been little Sadie between me and Violet, but she died back on the railroad tracks in Albert Lea. She was five years old when she walked into that train. I barely remembered her, but I put spring flowers on her grave a few times. We passed it on our way to the schoolhouse, back when Pearl, Bernie and I were all in one big classroom together, before moving to Minneapolis and everyone got some kind of angry.

Bernie would bring home something every day from the store, but not a lot of it. She'd bring home milk for Violet and sometimes brought bread and lard and coffee. Mama ate a little bread sometimes, but she just threw it up with her coffee in the morning. Her stomach was getting bigger though. I could see that.

A month had passed since Papa died and that's when Aunt Hattie showed up at our door. I recognized her from a photograph Mama kept in her bedroom and figured she was there because of those letters our landlady had sent out. Seeing her standing at our door holding a suitcase, I stopped myself from saying, "We don't need another mouth to feed here," but it's what I wanted to say.

Aunt Hattie barged right in and took control, barely saying hello to Pearl and Bernie and me, only asking, "Where's your mother?"

Pearl pointed her to Mama's bedroom in the back.

Aunt Hattie was yelling toward the back room as she walked, though we all knew Mama had just got done throwing up. She was lying in bed with Violet trying to play with her.

"Christina, come! Jeg tar deg hjem nå!"

That's all we heard because Aunt Hattie shut the bedroom door on all of us.

"Get, now! Out to the porch," Pearl was shooing Bernie and me.

"It's too cold," Bernie whined. I threw a shawl at her and tugged her out to the porch.

The elm trees were filling the street with leaves all up and down the block, but I saw no one on their porches. No one was walking to and from Lake Street and the streetcar stop. It was so quiet for the end of a work day.

"Pearl, are we going to go live with Aunt Hattie?" I finally asked as I hopped up onto the wide stone railing. It was cold without my own shawl.

"Be quiet, Gerty," Pearl said as she sat herself in a porch chair.

I saw Pearl and Bernie giving eyes to each other while they worked on some sewing on the underdrawers. Pearl got sewing from the Munsingwear Company downtown, riding the streetcar there and back every Friday to get paid for what she had finished and to pick up new work for the next week. She got a penny a piece for repairs to a pair of underdrawers, and two cents for attaching lace and ribbons to the prettier, new ones. She hadn't been making much money lately though because of the war. Nobody spent money on fancy underdrawers these days. Now, Mama being sick kept Pearl away from her sewing.

I swiveled my legs around on the stone wall to face down the street and leaned forward a little, trying to see if I could hear anything Aunt Hattie was saying to Mama, hoping something would come around the side of the house from Mama's back bedroom. Nothing did.

Down the block I noticed a black lorry pull up at the house of the German family who didn't speak English. Two men dressed all in white were carrying something up to the porch of the German house and then I couldn't see them anymore. A little later they came out carrying a long, black bag, one man on either end, and they appeared to be struggling because the bag was heavy. They put the bag in the back of their lorry and went back to the house. Soon they came out with another one, just like the first.

"Pearl, are the Germans moving away or something?" I asked without turning around.

Pearl got up to stand on the top step of the porch. She craned her neck down the street.

"Oh, dear. Looks like the Binders both died. What a shame," she said when she returned to her chair.

"They don't have any children at least," Bernie said.

"When's this Spanish Flu going to end anyway?" I asked, still watching the men at the lorry. At school, Mrs. Landry had said many more had died in the past week. "And why don't we just get it and die, too?"

"Gerty, how am I to know that? Do I look like a doctor?" Pearl broke some thread with her teeth.

"No, but you're always pretending like you know everything and you didn't even finish school." With my back to her, I felt brave enough to tease Pearl again.

Pearl had been doing piecework for as long as I could remember, since we moved to Minneapolis when I was only eight. She'd gone to school back in Albert Lea, but not here in the city. Mama said Pearl had to help with money because Papa drank so much, spending the cement mixing pay. Bernie, too, quit school in seventh grade. She'd been working at Josie's store since she was 15. I just knew I was probably smarter than both of them now, and I planned to graduate from high school no matter what. Mrs. Landry had told me that should be my goal. That's what she called it.

I could hear Aunt Hattie's deep voice shouting now. She had opened Mama's bedroom door.

"But the rent, Christine!" I heard her say.

Violet started screaming and pretty soon Aunt Hattie plopped her out onto the porch with us, without a sweater or anything.

"You girls watch your little sister now, you hear?" Aunt Hattie said. "Pearl, come with me."

Bernie took Violet onto her lap as Pearl followed Aunt Hattie back into the house. I don't know how long we stayed out on that porch, but it was starting to grow dark. One minute Aunt Hattie was back yelling at us all again. The next minute she had Mama by the elbow and had grabbed Violet in her other hand. Violet clung to the doll I had given her recently, the one Mama had made for me when I was Violet's age. Pearl stepped out to the porch, Mama's huge satchel in her hand, and suddenly the three of them were off down the porch steps, down the

20

street toward the Lake Street line, Bernie and I just staring after them, mouths open.

"Bye, Mama," Bernie called, tears streaming down her face.

Bye? That was all? I hopped down from the railing.

"Mama!" I screamed at her receding back. "Mama!"

"Oh, do shut up, Gerty," Bernie said as she plopped herself back onto a chair and wiped her eyes. "You're fifteen, for Pete's sakes. Don't make such a scene."

"Oh, you're one to talk, you big whiner," I said right back at her. I took some of Pearl's ribbons from the basket and twined them through my fingers.

Pearl came back down the street about 15 minutes later. Just Pearl. I saw her coming from about the German house, walking with her head down, walking real slow. I met her when she reached the porch steps.

"Violet, too? Oh, Pearl, I could have taken care of Violet," I told her. I kicked at the chair. Now I started to cry. No Violet. No more walking with her. No hearing her squeal. No playing blocks with her.

"Eth-el-lyn," Pearl said. "We can't all stay together anymore. We can't pay the rent."

"But when will Violet come home? It's only Mama who's sick."

"Mama and Violet are going to live with Aunt Hattie now."

"But, you know I could have taken care of Violet. You know it."

"We'll just have to see, Ethelyn. We've just got to wait and see." Pearl said. "Bernie and I will be working. You'll be in school. Maybe when Violet is old enough for school..."

"Nobody asked me!" I screamed at the two of them. I threw Pearl's ribbons at her.

We all just stood there looking at each other, trying not to look at each other. It was like the day Papa died. Silent. Frozen in place. The cold wind was picking up. Pearl finally ordered us all into the house.

"We've just got to wait and see."

CHAPTER 4

Wait and see. I'm sure not going to wait and see. I'm going to do something. I'll walk to Albert Lea, that's what I'll do.

In bed that night Mama left, when Pearl and Bernie thought I was asleep, the two of them got up and went into Mama's now empty bedroom. I followed them a few minutes later and stood listening through the closed door.

"Aunt Hattie told me that Aunt Sigrid's going to let the two of us work for her at the lumberjack camp, but she can't pay our way up there. Aunt Hattie will send us train tickets to Brooten as soon as she gets down to Albert Lea and gets her crops in," Pearl was saying. "The tickets will be here in a week or so."

I could just tell Pearl had been holding onto this secret bit of news since Aunt Hattie had called her back into Mama's room this afternoon. The two of them had made plans for Bernie and Pearl, but what about me?

"Do you think I can be a waitress for her? I want to be a waitress." I could hear Bernie say.

"I guess so. The lumberjacks gotta have somebody feeding them," Pearl said. "I guess I'll be doing the washing."

"I wish Violet was with us," Bernie said.

"You know we can't work and take care of her, too."

"I guess. But an orphanage? That's just awful, ain't it?"

An orphanage? I couldn't believe what I was hearing.

"Aunt Hattie says it's real close by. Mama will get to visit Violet when she recovers after the baby," Pearl said.

"Mama will at least have the new baby when she gets well."

"Now, Mrs. Jordahl is going to be asking questions soon about paying the rent. We'll just tell her Mama's being taken care of and will be back here real soon, when she's better. We're not going to mention the baby, remember that. We'll take the night train and Mrs. Jordahl won't see us go."

"Can I take all my dresses, do you think?" Bernie asked. Leave it to Bernie. Always worried about her stupid looks.

"One bag. Whatever you can fit," Pearl answered. "Now, the county lady's going to be here at noon tomorrow when Gerty's back from school for lunch. Aunt Hattie got that all settled, too. It's one less person for everyone to worry about, having her at the county school. They'll take care of her. That's what they do there. We better start cleaning up and packing tomorrow after Gerty goes, so we're ready when our tickets come."

One less person for everybody to worry about? So that's what I am now. An extra person. I am the one that makes it too many mouths to feed around here!

I heard them get up from Mama's squeaky bed and I had to scramble back to our bedroom. I got the covers over myself just in time.

When my breathing slowed down, a thought occurred to me. School? What did Pearl mean when she said county school? What's wrong with my own school? I wondered. Well, I'm not sticking around to find out, that's what. I made my own plans, seething there in the dark as those two got to sleep. I'll go off to school tomorrow and never come back. They'll see I can make my own decisions, better ones than that ol' Aunt Hattie cooked up for me.

I told myself to wake up early, so I don't think I really slept the rest of the night. Pearl was always the first awake, and Bernie got to the store early on Mondays, so I knew I'd have to be careful. My leaving had to be timed just right and so quiet! If I grabbed the bag from under my bed and my dresses from the peg, I could stuff them in as I walked down the sidewalk. I'd be down the street at the first hint of morning.

I had only one nickel in my box of treasures. I grabbed the dresses from my peg. The treasure box was the last thing I took with the morning light getting brighter through our shades.

The streetcar pulled up just as I reached Lake Street and I hopped on toward South Middle School. The rail yards were in the opposite direction, but I knew I had to go to school to make it look right. This driver knew me, knew school was the other way. All the windows on the streetcar were open even though it was a cold morning. I had left my ragged old coat behind.

"You're early today, miss," the driver said to me when I climbed down his steps at the school stop.

"Special project," I answered, lifting my bag and treasure box to show him they were some part of it.

The schoolyard was empty as I figured it would be. I prayed that a teacher or somebody had unlocked the school door though. I wanted to get a drink at the water fountain just inside. It might make me less hungry. I found a hand-written sign on butcher paper tacked to the big front door of the school.

"School cancelled until further notice because of the sickness," it said. I looked around.

Would Pearl and Bernie know about this? Probably not, I decided. I'd gone to school just last Friday. How could they know? I turned myself toward Minnehaha Avenue, toward the grain elevators where Kjersti and I used to play and watch the trains get loaded when we first moved here. I know people rode the trains for free all the time. I had seen some of the men waving at us from the cars going by, and I had seen some of them booted off by policemen at the stop. Those men didn't have any money or food either. I guess they didn't have any family to watch out for them. Just like me now.

The walk was one Kjersti and I had done many times, maybe ten blocks. Not long. I carried the bag of dresses under my arm, crushing them, and walked carefully around the piles of rocks and sacks of flour near the grain elevators. A little shack stood empty near the tracks. I found a stack of wooden carriage wheels around the corner of the grain building and waited there, tucked down behind them and listening for a train to come from St. Paul. When it did, I was going to jump on without anyone seeing me.

The platform was totally empty and quiet. A depot manager usually stood in that little shack, I knew. He must be around here somewhere. I examined my boots, worried they wouldn't let me run fast when the time came. I never could run fast. One heel was nearly worn down and it made me limp.

I felt the train's approach before I heard it, but just then I noticed a policeman checking doors down at the other end of the long building. I ducked quickly back

26

around behind the carriage wheels, then went all the way around the street side of the building to come out at the far end, the opposite direction the policeman had been heading. By the time I reached the other end, the train was in sight, slowing down. As it came nearer, I walked into the bushes along the tracks, the way it had come, looking for an open door on one of the cars. With a glance back toward the engine that had just passed, I made sure the engineer couldn't see me. I would have to hop on the minute it stopped, before the man in the caboose could stick his head out, like they always did.

I got lucky. The train stopped with the seventh car right in front of me, and there was an open door. I checked on the policeman's progress. Not there. Nobody. Hoisting the bag under one arm, I ran as fast as I could up to the box car's open door, but stopped. It was way over my head. I stepped back, tossed my bag into it and took a standing jump. My elbows got hooked onto the car floor, but it turned out to be slippery. I fell back, the wind knocked out of me, flat-backed in the sooty dirt.

"Whoa there, young lady, what do you think you are doing?"

The policeman stood over me, upside down in my eyes.

"Nothing," I said, glancing up at the bag peeking from the boxcar's edge. My elbow was all scraped up and I had landed in something like coal dust.

"Get up now and come with me," the policeman said.

I tried to stand and brush off my dress and boots. The policeman grabbed my elbow to help me and said, "Where's your papa now?"

"Dead," I answered, trying to get my elbow free from the man.

"Your mama?"

"Gone."

"You live around here?"

"We're moving," I said.

"Who's we, now?'

"Me and my sisters."

"And where might they be, now?" the policeman asked.

I knew if I told him he would make me go home.

"Working," I said.

"Shouldn't you be in school then?"

"School's closed."

"Sounds like you gotta tell me where to find these sisters of yours then, or else I have to bring you to jail."

Jail? Papa was there once, and Mama had had to go get him. I didn't know where jail was.

"I live by Josie's store," I finally answered.

"Come on then. Let's go." He pulled at my elbow again and moved to grab my bag. I struggled to get away so I could get my treasure box from the boxcar.

"I have to get that," I pointed. He let me go.

The heel had broken off my other boot so I didn't limp now. I rubbed my free elbow and grabbed the box down. We walked the eight blocks away from the grain elevators, toward Josie's store, towards home. Along the way, the policeman said he was sorry to hear my papa had died.

"Lots of that happening," he said. "My brother, too. Heard they're shutting down theaters and dances today. I'll be downtown tonight, sure, to be keeping the peace."

I didn't answer him. I was mad to the bone and worried about what Pearl would do when I showed up at our house with a policeman. Maybe I won't show him the right house, I thought, but as we passed the house where the Germans had lived, empty now, I couldn't think what I would say if I said that house was mine and no one answered the door.

I led the policeman around to our side door and Pearl and Bernie jumped up from the kitchen table, both still in their nightdresses with their hair down in big long messes.

"Ethelyn, where did you go?" Pearl yanked at my elbow.

"I'm not going with no county lady anywhere," I said and got myself free. I plopped on a chair.

"I'm sorry if she caused you trouble," Pearl said to the policeman. "Thank you, officer. We can take care of her."

"You ladies all alone here?" the policeman asked.

"For now, but my sister and I are moving up north soon. Our Mama's sick," Pearl said.

"What about this one?" The policeman jerked his head toward me.

"The county says she'll stay in school here. A lady's coming by later today to bring her there. A Mrs. McAuliff."

"Yes. Good. You need any help?"

"No, sir. Thank you. We'll be fine."

The policeman turned to me.

"Don't go hopping on any more trains now, you hear? Bad things happen to girls like you out there."

I just glared at the man and grabbed some bread from the cupboard.

Pearl walked the policeman to the front door and when she came back she yelled.

"Gerty, this is the way it's got to be now, so try to be a grown-up for once and behave," she said. "We're in a lot of trouble and hopping trains is not going to help anything. They can send you to jail for that, you know. You're lucky to be going to a school."

"Why can't I go with you two?" I yelled back before stuffing some bread in my mouth.

"There is no work for you, and no room, Aunt Sigrid says. We'll send you money and Mama will write, and we'll write to you."

"Yeah, you barely know how to write," I said. "I could have gone with Mama to help take care of Violet. Nobody even asked me." I was yelling now and fighting to keep from crying.

"You must mind your manners. I am in charge now, Mama said so. I see you already took your dresses, you little brat. Now you go into our room right now and get the rest of your things in order. The lady will be here at noon."

Bernie and Pearl had already put my things onto my bed. I sat and looked around the room. I missed having Violet sleeping in her cradle in the corner. Violet in an orphanage. That sounds just terrible, especially when she's got a family. What kind of school lets you to live there? I couldn't picture it. I'm sure the boys and girls there will be horrible and not anywhere near smart enough. Mama living with Aunt Hattie, a baby coming. Bernie and Pearl off way up north, working. I pushed all of my things onto the floor, held my box of treasures to my chest and lay down and cried.

"Ethelyn!"

I woke up to Pearl calling my name. My real name. She had a kind of sing-song in her voice, too happy.

"Come out here and meet Mrs. McAuliff." Pearl was standing at the bedroom door now. "Come now."

Mrs. McAuliff was sitting in the one good chair in the front room, where Papa had sat reading newspapers on the evenings he was home. Bernie sat on the kitchen chair she had pulled in. Pearl asked Mrs. McAuliff if she would like coffee.

"Thank you, dear, no," the woman said as I came out from behind Pearl. "This must be our Ethelyn?"

Mrs. McAuliff stood up.

"I'm so happy you'll be joining our little family at the school. You will love the other girls," she said.

I said nothing, but I glared at Pearl and Bernie.

"My, what has happened to your heels, dear?" Mrs. McAuliff was looking at my boots.

I had forgotten how broken they now were without heels, my toes kind of pointed up in the air. I didn't have another pair to wear anyway. "They broke," I said.

"Well, we're going to take good care of you and if you work real hard at Home School, you'll earn some new boots in no time."

"Work?" I said.

"Certainly. All our girls earn things at the school by working--laundry and canning and such. You'll have fun and meet some girls as nice as your sisters here."

That was just about the most wrong thing for her to say.

"They're not nice," I said. "They didn't even ask me. They sent my little sister away."

Pearl and Bernie ignored my comment. Pearl put on her fake smile, all nice and polite with the lady.

"Ethelyn, you must run along with Mrs. McAuliff now. We have the address and we'll write you a note the minute we get to Aunt Sigrid's. And Mama will write to you when she's well."

She stepped over to try to hug me, Bernie following right behind her, but I shrugged out from under them. I moved over to the front door and went out onto the porch.

"Goodbye," I said, looking out onto the deserted street.

Mrs. McAuliff said something to Pearl who then handed my bag and treasure box to the lady.

"Now then, a little walk to the streetcar and we'll be on our way. It isn't far, really. It's over by the brewery. Do you know where that is?"

She told me to carry my things and handed them to me. She pulled on brown gloves and buttoned them.

Of course I knew where the brewery was. I had been there, enough to know that when we boarded the streetcar, we were heading toward downtown, not Polish Town where the brewery was and where this school was supposed to be. It was the downtown line, moving toward the tall buildings I planned to shop in one day. Young Quinlan. Donaldson's. I had seen them when Papa had taken us to a candy shop near the Milwaukee Road Depot, once when he had some extra money. That must have been on Bernie's birthday or after Violet had been born. Was Mrs. McAuliff taking me to the shops before going to the school?

"Here's our stop, dear," Mrs. McAuliff announced as the car pulled up to a red stone building that was nearly the biggest one downtown. She brushed at some of the coal dust still on my dress and we stepped up to the sidewalk.

"We have to look nice, don't we, for the judge?" she said as she brushed.

"Judge?" I said.

"Yes, dear, he has to say it's fine for you to go to our school."

"I thought my sisters already said that," I said. "I sure didn't."

"Now, don't be impolite. We just have to make it official and all. You know there are so many girls in trouble these days."

"I'm not in trouble. My Papa died."

"Yes, Ethelyn, and I'm sorry. We just have to be grown up now and do what's best for everybody, don't we?"

She turned my shoulder toward the big stone building.

"What's best would be letting me go to my Mama and little sister," I said.

We stepped inside a cold and dark entryway lined with stained glass windows on either side of the door. It felt like a church only without the musty smell. The floor was polished stone and slippery. Inside further was a big lobby with a tall flower pot in the middle, filled with orange and yellow flowers taller than any I'd ever seen.

33

All around were heavy, wooden doors that looked like a painting of a king's castle I remembered from the school library.

Mrs. McAuliff led me to one of the doors on the right. It had a gold plaque on the door, "Judge Waite."

Mrs. McAuliff pushed the door open. Inside was brighter and warmer and a lady in a dark blue, satin dress, with a pearl brooch at her throat, sat at a wooden desk facing us.

"Hello, Mrs. McAuliff," the lady said. "Who do we have here?"

"Another one of our school girls," Mrs. McAuliff said. "The judge is expecting us at two. Say hello, Ethelyn."

I had been staring at the telephone machine on the woman's desk. I had seen pictures of telephone machines, but had never seen one for real.

"Hello," I said, though I didn't take my eyes off the machine.

"Go on in, Mrs. McAuliff. He's just now ready for you."

We went through another wooden door and inside was even more wood, all around the room, and at the front was a high dark bench. I thought of church again, all quiet. Behind the bench sat a man in a black robe talking to a lady in a brown dress and they were looking at some papers together.

"Mrs. McAuliff. Come in." The man motioned with his fountain pen for us to come closer.

"Thank you, your honor. We're here for a commitment today. Again," Mrs. McAuliff said.

"We've seen quite a bit of you lately, Mrs. McAuliff. And who do you have with you today?"

He said something to the lady bending over his desk and she went out a door behind him.

"I have Ethelyn today, your honor. Her father died. Ethelyn Gertrude Thompson."

"Step up, step up," the judge said, again motioning us forward.

"Hello, Evelyn," the judge said.

"It's Ethelyn," I said.

"Eth-el-lyn, then. My apologies. How old are you?"

"Fifteen."

Mrs. McAuliff leaned toward my ear. "Say 'Fifteen, your honor', dear."

"Fifteen, your honor."

I looked down at my boots and thought about stomping on Mrs. McAuliff's foot.

"Fifteen. Well, I'm so happy I'll be seeing you over at our little school, Ethelyn. Mrs. Waite and I come by there quite often."

I didn't know if I should say anything.

"Who brings this committal process?" the judge asked as he sat up straight and looked at Mrs. McAuliff.

"Her aunt, mother and sisters, your honor. The sisters are of age."

"And why can't they take care of her, Mrs. McAuliff?" the judge asked.

"She is somewhat incorrigible, your honor. She was out to the railroad tracks this morning. There is little money." At this, Mrs. McAuliff reached down and started brushing at my dress again. I pushed her hand away.

35

"And they are moving out of the area to find work. Her mother is sick and has had to move south, in with a sister. In the family way, too, I am led to understand."

"And how old are the sisters?"

"They're 22 and 20, your honor, and have found lodgings with another aunt up north, in a lumberjack camp."

The judge shook his head. "I don't care for the stories I've been reading in the papers about how girls are treated at those lumber camps. Shame really."

"Yes, your honor," Mrs. McAuliff said. "Still, there's paying work, room and board."

"Well, let's do what we can to keep this one in school. She'll learn a trade? Or work out as a domestic, I presume? Is that the plan?"

"I would assume so, your honor. We'll give her all the tests."

I tried to memorize the words I heard. Incorrigible. Domestic. I'll look them up at that stupid school if it has a dictionary.

"Are there health problems?"

"None that I know of, your honor."

"Fine, then, but we'll order a t.b. check, of course. I'll be seeing you at the school, Ethelyn." The judge was looking at me, but I said nothing. He wrote something and handed Mrs. McAuliff a piece of paper.

"Thank you, your honor. There's another tomorrow," she said as she took the paper from him.

"Oh, I don't doubt that in the least," he said, laughing. "You are bound and determined to keep us busy here, aren't you?"

He turned to talk with the brown-dressed woman again.

"Come on, dear," Mrs. McAuliff said to me. She tried to take my hand, but I pulled it away from her.

"I am not a baby," I said and I walked back up to the door we had come in, Mrs. McAuliff behind me.

Out on the street, Mrs. McAuliff said, "You really must learn to be more polite, Ethelyn. It's not becoming to be sullen with the judge."

A streetcar pulled up and that kept me from answering her. I carried my satchel of dresses and other things, my treasure box in my other arm. I followed Mrs. McAuliff into the streetcar with a sign by the door that said, "Northeast."

"What is 'incorrigible'," I asked Mrs. McAuliff when we found our seat.

"I can't explain that now dear. It's a legal term you wouldn't understand."

She held the judge's paper in her lap and on it I could see my name, written out by the judge, and a line where he had also written, "Hennepin County Home School for Girls."

Stamped over this in big red letters it said "Inmate."

CHAPTER 5

We got off the streetcar in front of the huge Grain Belt Brewery that I recognized. We walked to the right, passing an empty baseball park. At the other side of it we turned up the walk of a house that looked like it belonged on a farm, the type surrounding Albert Lea where we used to live. A farmhouse here, just a few streetcar stops from those tall buildings downtown? It was an ugly gray and it needed paint. It sat far back from the street in the middle of a browning garden, its plants drooping and turning yellow. Bees buzzed around some fading flowers.

Five girls were in front of the house, all wearing matching dresses that weren't at all pretty. They looked like the flour sacks I had seen this morning stacked to be loaded at the railroad yard. Was that only this morning? Two of the girls were hanging wash on a line and the other three raked leaves into a pile that was smoking.

Mrs. McAuliff led me up a path through the garden that turned out to be full of cucumbers. At the end of the garden, nearest the house, a man in overalls bent over some of the plants, picking beetles off of them and dropping them into a jar. He stood up tall when he noticed Mrs. McAuliff.

"M'am," he said, as we passed.

"Hello, Henry," Mrs. McAuliff said. "This here is Ethelyn."

"Hello Ett-lynn. Velcome," he said. He sounded a little like Mr. Binder, the German man who had died.

We stepped into a front room that looked like ours at home, only much bigger with lots more chairs. The big farmhouse was dark and cold. A huge stone fireplace on the opposite wall was not burning. The battered chairs were lined up against the wall on three sides. The house smelled like the ammonia Mama used for cleaning. No one was in the room, but we could hear girls talking and laughing in the back somewhere.

I followed Mrs. McAuliff toward the sounds and we stepped into a bright white room filled with washtubs and scrubbing boards on one side and a stove and ironing board on the other. Three girls stood around pushing each other, but they stopped when they noticed Mrs. McAuliff.

"Girls, now get back to your work. This is Ethelyn. You'll meet her at supper."

We passed through the big room quickly to a side door and went up some carpeted steps, stopping at the first door on the right.

"You'll be here," Mrs. McAuliff said.

Inside the room were four cots, two on the right and two on the left, head-to-head. Between the beds was a row of four pegs and four hard chairs under them. The pegs were filled with clothes. Each bed was made and covered with a flour sack blanket that looked a lot like the dresses the girls downstairs were wearing. Two dressers were against the opposite wall.

Mrs. McAuliff showed me which bed was to be mine and said I could use one drawer in a dresser for my under things. One drawer, like the bureau I shared with Bernie and Pearl at home. Home. This was going to be my home now? I sat on my bed and started to cry.

"Now, stop. You're too old for that now, aren't you? Remember it's you who said you were not a baby?" Mrs.

McAuliffe stood over me with her arms crossed on her chest.

"I've seen grown-ups cry, you know," I said.

"Here at Home School, you get points taken away for talking back. I'm taking two of your points. Only two, since you're new today, but usually it will be five. The more points you lose, the longer it will take you to earn those boots you need. Now, remember that."

"I don't care about boots. I want to be with my mama."

"It seems your mama can't be with you and I'm starting to understand why she might not want to be."

She opened one of the dresser drawers.

"Under things only in here. Everything else goes on the peg. One peg, you understand?"

She pointed out a peg that already had clothes on it, but there was a little sign over it with my full name spelled out. "Ethelyn Gertrude Thompson".

"Those girls," Mrs. McAuliff said, and she took the clothes on the peg and moved them to the next one over. She reached through them and pulled out one item.

"Now, hush. Here's your dress for the week. There's a different one for Sunday, which you'll get on Saturday from Mrs. Hansen. I'll give that dirty thing you are wearing to Mrs. Hansen and you put this on after a wash in the tub down the hall."

She handed me the dress that looked just like the ones all the girls in the front yard had been wearing.

"Supper is at five, when you hear the bell. Just follow the other girls. I'll leave you now."

Good, I thought, but knew better than to say out loud. I couldn't believe I felt hungry, but I'd only had the bread from the cupboard this morning.

"Is there any bread?" I thought to ask Mrs. McAuliff before she went out the door.

"You get bread at supper. Now wash," she said and closed the door behind her.

There was no clock in the room. I didn't know how long it was until 5 o'clock, but then I remembered my treasure box had Mama's special silver watch in it, the one she gave me for my confirmation at church last spring. "To Ethelyn. Love Mother" it said on the back.

I was only allowed to wear it on special occasions, Mama had told me. We hadn't had any special occasions since then. Losing one's family and being forced to live with strangers seemed like a special occasion to me, so I put it on. Mama wasn't there to tell me no, or Pearl or Bernie neither. The watch was not telling the right time. I had not wound it lately, though I took it out of the box at home once in a while in case I was going to wear it. Just as I got it clasped on my wrist, I heard a bell ring outside and went to the one window in the bedroom. Outside I saw an old, brown building that must be a church, at an angle to the house's back yard. I counted. The bell rang four times. One full hour until supper. I set the watch to the right time and wound it.

Down the hall was a toilet room with white and black tile on the floor and a sink that was like a laundry sink, the one in our cellar at home, only longer. I closed the door and took off my dress. A little rag hung on a peg next to the sink and I held it under the faucet. Warm running water indoors. We didn't have that at home.

41

After cleaning myself, I put the new dress on and it scratched through my underclothes. I took the wet rag to get some of the coal dust off my sooty, broken boots. It made the rag black and the black wouldn't wash out under the water.

A tall girl pushed the door open suddenly and she saw the dirty rag in my hand.

"Hey, what have you done with our washcloth? Look what you did," and she snatched the rag from me. "We won't get a new one until Saturday, you stupid little brat."

She was a lot taller than me and had very black hair that was in one long thick braid down her back. Her stomach pouched out from her dress.

"I'm sorry," I said. "My name is Ethelyn and I'm new."

"Ha. I heard your name was Gerty, so which is it?"

"It's not Gerty. It's Ethelyn. Whoever said Gerty is lying." I picked up my things from the floor.

"Everybody here lies," the girl said. "Are you calling me a liar?" She threw the rag hard back into the sink and looked at me hard.

"No. I just wanted you to know my right name." I wanted to get out of there fast and turned toward the door.

"Liars. They told me I'd get to be home by now. Am I home? Hell, no." But she wasn't looking at me any more, she was talking to herself in the mirror over the sink. I didn't know what to say so I just left, saying nothing, and went back down the hall to the bedroom.

"Gerty, Gerty," the girl called after me. Then she slammed the bathroom door.

In my bag with the dresses I had stuffed into it early that morning I found my remaining set of underdrawers and one pair of stockings. I also found the two framed photographs from my dresser at home. One was a portrait of me in my confirmation dress, holding the Bible we were all given. Pastor Torkelson had made me sit real still at the church for that.

Pearl had taken that beautiful dress and made underdrawers out of it in September, saying we all needed new ones come winter and fabric was still hard to get with the war. The other picture was of Mama and her two sisters, Aunt Hattie and Aunt Sigrid, before they were all married, all of them wearing the same old-fashioned, high-collared dress. Pearl, Bernie and I had each been given this picture one Christmas.

I set the two pictures on top of the dresser and stuffed my other things in the drawer. The underdrawers and stockings didn't take up half of it. I tried hanging my two dresses from home on the peg below my name card, but they just slid off, so I stuffed them in the drawer with the under things. I looked around, not knowing what to do next, so I lay down on the bed and straightened out my dress. It was going to get so wrinkled, the fabric was stiff as paper.

I guess I fell asleep and I woke up when I heard a bell different from the church bell. It was the kind Mrs. Landry rang to call us students from the schoolyard. I heard girls running past the door, so I got up and opened it to find a black-skinned girl going past.

"Supper!" the girl shouted, and I got behind her quick and followed her downstairs.

We all went into a room off the front room with six big tables, each set with bowls and spoons. There were so many girls now I wondered where they all had come from. Were there no boys here? Nobody was talking, so I followed the dark girl and stood next to her when she stopped at one chair in front of one bowl.

"You can't sit here. New girls are in front. You're new."

The girl gave me a little push toward the front table, just as Mrs. McAuliff came in the side door.

"Ethelyn, you're to come up with me." And she took my hand like a baby's.

All the girls were now standing behind a chair at a table, and Mrs. McAuliff turned me around at the front of the room.

"Girls, we have Ethelyn here now. Ethelyn Gertrude Thomas."

"Gerty!" I heard someone at the back of the room shout out and saw it was the older girl from the wash room who had said it. The other girls with her at that table all giggled.

"Dorethea. Hush."

"Ethelyn will be glad to meet you all later in the front room, won't you Ethelyn?" And she smiled at me, patted my shoulder.

I didn't think I was supposed to say anything.

"Ethelyn, say hello." Mrs. McAuliff jostled her shoulder.

"Hello," I said. "I'm not Gerty."

All the girls in the back now laughed out loud.

"No, you're not. You're Ethelyn. Now stand here."

"My name is Rosie," she said. "Short for Roselyn, so our names are kind of the same. They end in "Lyn". Ethel-lyn. See?"

"Yes," I said.

"What do you want to sew?" she asked.

"I don't know how."

"Oh. I guess they'll teach you then. It helps you to sew things. You get points. Do you want me to teach you?" Rosie asked.

I didn't really, but since I couldn't see any books in the room, I agreed. "Yes, please."

Rosie had a pair of long stockings in her hand and she showed me the hole in one toe.

"There are always stockings to mend," she said. "My grandma taught me before she died. I lived with my grandma before they brought me here."

"Did she have the sickness? The Spanish flu?" I asked.

"No. She was just old and died. My mama died when she had a baby. That was last year. The baby died, too."

"My mama's going to have a baby," I told her, though I wasn't sure if I was supposed to for some reason.

"Is that why you're here?" Rosie asked.

"I don't know why I'm here. Mama went away with Violet, my little sister. My older sisters sent me here."

"Too many mouths to feed." Rosie nodded. "Lots of girls are here because there were too many mouths to feed. Me, I'm just an orphan. And some of the girls are here because they're going to have babies."

"Girls are having babies?" I asked. I was surprised.

"Some of them. Bergit? Who sat next to you at supper? She's having a baby. And Dorethea, the mean one with the long braid? Some others, too."

Now I understood about the milk. Bergit had gotten more milk from the kitchen lady because the baby in her stomach needed it. I looked around the room trying to guess now which girls were having babies.

"Will the babies live here when they are born?" I whispered to Rosie.

"No. We never see any of the babies. The girls go across town to the infirmary for a week, then they come back without the baby. Or we don't see the girl again neither. Sometimes. It just depends."

Rosie kept sewing while she was talking, forgetting to show me how, which was fine. Rosie bit the thread with her teeth and started tying knots.

"Do you play baseball?" Rosie asked with her mouth full of thread.

"Baseball? No," I said. "We didn't have any boys around to teach us how."

"Us girls can teach you. On Saturdays we play. You'll see."

Baseball and sewing? I liked the idea of knowing what was going to happen next. I would learn new things. I hoped this school didn't have arithmetic. Mrs. Landry was always saying how smart I was, but not in arithmetic. It was not my strong suit, she had said.

"Gerty, where are you from?" I looked up to see a tall girl who was very skinny standing in front of Rosie and me. She didn't have her two front teeth and what teeth she did have were all crooked.

"My name is Ethelyn," I said to her, clenching my own teeth.

"Yeah, Judy, it's Ethelyn--like Roselyn--so stop making fun of her," Rosie said to the tall girl.

"I ain't making fun. They said that was her name," Judy answered.

"It's Ethelyn," I said again.

"Okay, Ethy. Can you catch a ball? For baseball, I mean?" The tall girl put her hands on her hips as she watched me.

"I don't know. I can bounce one."

"That doesn't really work for baseball. What else can you do?"

"I can play jacks. And do the Cat's Cradle?" I offered.

"What's that?" Judy asked.

"You need string. Do you have any string?" I asked.

"I've got yarn here," Judy said, and she pulled a long strand from the pocket of her dress.

"That will work." I took the gray yarn from her.

I told Rosie to put the stockings down and I grabbed her two hands, winding the yarn over and through them like Bernie and I had done hundreds of times a few summers ago. I weaved the web and then took the strands from Rosie's fingers onto my own.

"See," I said, holding my hands out for Judy to see. "You just make new patterns."

"Let me try," Judy said and she took a chair from nearby and pulled it over.

For the rest of the evening, I taught some of the girls who soon gathered around to watch. Five of them had put down their sewing. The three oldest girls who had sat in the back of the dining room and called me Gerty looked over once and sing-songed at us, "Babies doing baby games," but Rosie and the others ignored them.

I heard the church bell bong out nine times and then Mrs. Hansen, the big lady who had cleaned up the spilled milk, came into the room and yelled.

"Bed! Bed! You go now!" She flapped her apron at us.

All the girls put their things away in their baskets and stored them under their chairs. Since I didn't have a basket, I wondered where and when I would ever get one.

I was unhappy when I learned Rosie was not one of the girls in my bedroom, but upstairs in our beds, my head was up close to Bergit's. We whispered together like Bernie and Pearl had always done without me. I told Bergit how just that morning I had tried to hop on a train and how it seemed like that was many weeks ago.

"I wish someone had told me how long I am supposed to stay here," I whispered in the dark. "That judge didn't say a thing about it. Mrs. McAuliff either. How long will you stay here?"

"'Until I'm 17, next year. Don't know where I go then though," Bergit said. "They never tell us anything. Sometimes we wake up to find two or three girls gone in one day, no good-byes, but sometimes it's good riddance."

She giggled.

"But won't you get to go back to your family after the baby comes?"

"Got none," she said. "I guess I'll be a maid or something. Mrs. McAuliff sees to that for all of us."

A maid, I thought. I don't want to be a maid, though I wasn't sure what one did exactly. Nobody I knew had a maid.

"You'll get your school book tomorrow. We have to go to chapel first, then breakfast, then school. It's like that every day. So boring," Bergit was saying.

"Is Mrs. McAuliff the teacher?"

"No, Miss Johnson. And Mrs. Arnold on Wednesday, for arithmetic."

I groaned, but suddenly felt very sleepy.

"Ethelyn?" I heard Bergit say.

"Shut up, you two!" Dorethea yelled from her bed on the other side of the room.

"Shut up yourself, Dorethea," Bergit yelled and then she threw her pillow right over at Dorethea. "I sure can't wait til you and your stupid baby go away."

Somebody pounded on our bedroom door.

"Quiet in there girls! I take your points a-vay."

Bergit and I got to giggling again at the way Mrs. Hansen said "a-vay" instead of "away."

Dorethea threw Bergit's pillow back at her, but I couldn't keep my eyes from closing. I thought about how the policeman pulled me up from the dust that morning, which made me smile, and then I didn't think anything else.

CHAPTER 6

Dear Mama,

This is my first morning at Home School. After breakfast this morning, I got to go to a little room and get a tablet of paper that will be all mine for school, and that's what I'm writing in here. I'll tear out these pages later. I hope I save enough for my lessons because I don't think they'll give me another tablet until spring or maybe at Christmas. Karen said so. She's one of the other girls in my room.

This school stinks of ammonia and lye and something like pickles when I go near the kitchen. They said I'm supposed to learn how to make pickles on Friday, so I guess that's why it smells that way. I don't know why they don't just go to the store and buy pickles, like the ones Bernie used to bring home.

It's crowded in our room and two of the girls don't care where they put their things. They use up all the pegs. That Dorethea girl says it's her right because she's been here longest. I don't like her one bit. Karen says Dorethea will be gone soon. Her baby will come and she'll go away.

Karen's Mama died and her daddy is in jail. Karen stole a lot of bread and cheese and lived in a shack for a while. That's why she's here. She's shy and I like her, but she's also leaving soon, so why bother trying to be friends with her? Maybe I can come live with you soon and help you with the baby when it comes?

The last girl in my room is Bergit who is also going to have a baby. Rosie says lots of the girls here are going to have babies but you can't ever tell because of these stupid dresses we wear, like bags. Bergit used to live on a farm down by Iowa and she doesn't know if she will get to go back there. Her baby will go away to some Minneapolis family. Bergit won't even see her baby when it's born.

We had some kind of porridge for breakfast and a plate of sliced tomatoes because the girls said that's what they picked in the garden yesterday. We'll eat nothing but squash pretty soon, Karen says, even for breakfast. I guess there's a cow and chickens, too.

I remember Pearl feeding chickens in our yard in Albert Lea. I haven't been to the back yard yet to the chicken house and the stall for the cows. Rosie told me she hates feeding the chickens because they go after your feet. I don't think I want to milk a cow either, but I don't think I have any choice. Do you think you can write me a letter soon, when you feel better, I mean?

This morning before breakfast we had to have church in the sitting room. They called it chapel. Karen said we do this every day. Mrs. McAuliff made us sing but I didn't know the words and they didn't give us any books to sing from like we did when I went to church for confirmation. Remember that, Mama? I am wearing the watch you gave me, though it's not really a special occasion. I hope you aren't mad. I think about you every time I wind it.

Mrs. McAuliffe sang up at the front of the room this morning and only one other girl sang, too. She looked like she was trying to impress Mrs. McAuliffe, but I liked the big blue bow in her hair. Mama, I would like to get my hair cut here. Do you think I can? Did Aunt Hattie tell you about this school, because Bernie and Pearl said she was the one who decided I should come here, since you were sick.

We have school at 10 o'clock, so I have to stop writing now.

I heard the school bell ringing downstairs and tore the letter out of the notebook and tucked it under my pillow.

CHAPTER 7

All the girls hurried to the dining room again, but now all the chairs faced the front and we girls crammed into one side of the tables to face Mrs. McAuliff and a lady I hadn't seen before.

"Girls, it's Tuesday so you know this is the day we start with reading. Miss Johnson will teach you until it's time for lunch and chores. You will read for her when she asks you to."

Mrs. McAuliff frowned at Dorethea at the back, then nodded at Miss Johnson and left the room.

"Good morning, girls," Miss Johnson said. She wore a pretty gingham dress and was a lot younger than Mrs. Landry at my old school.

"Good morning, Miss Johnson," all the girls said together, except me.

"Do any of you remember whose turn it is to read this morning?"

Rosie raised her hand.

"Yes, Rosie, it is your turn. You read and then we'll ask Ethelyn here to be next. All right, Ethelyn?"

"Gerty!" one of the older girls sitting in the back said.

"Quiet in the back," Miss Johnson said. "Go ahead, Rosie."

Rosie stood up and Miss Johnson gave her a book that was open. "Start here, please."

Rosie read:

Early one morning Grandmother Grey got up, opened the windows and doors of the farmhouse, and soon everybody on the place was stirring. The cook hurried breakfast, and no sooner was it over than

Grandfather Grey went out to the barn and hitched the two horses to the wagon.

"Get up, Robin and Dobbin!" he said, as he drove through the big gate. "If you knew who were coming back in this wagon you would not be stepping so slowly."

The old horses pricked up their ears when they heard this, and trotted away as fast as they could down the country road until they came to town. Just as they got to the railway station the train came whizzing in.

"All off!" cried the conductor, as the train stopped; and out came a group of children who were, every one of them, Grandfather and Grandmother Grey's grandchildren. They had come to spend Thanksgiving Day on the farm.

There was John, who was named for grandfather and looked just like him, and the twins, Teddie and Pat, who looked like nobody but each other; their papa was grandfather's oldest son. Then there was Louisa, who had a baby sister at home, and then Mary Virginia Martin, who was her mamma's only child.

"I tell you," said grandfather, as he helped them into the wagon, "your grandmother will be glad to see you!"*

"Very good, Rosie." Miss Johnson stopped her.

"Now girls, this is a story about a farm, isn't it?

Has anyone here lived on a farm before this school?"

Bergit's hand went up, and many of the others raised their hands, too.

"Yes, Bergit, where was your farm?"

"I don't know, Miss Johnson," she said. The girls in back giggled at this.

"Was it far from here?"

"I guess so. Yes. We were on the train a long time to get here."

"Did you have pigs, Bergit?"

"No, ma'am, we had cows, two of them. And lots of corn in the summer."

"Did you sell the corn or eat it?"

"Ate it, ma'am. That's what we ate all summer."

"Did you help to plant the corn, Bergit?"

"No ma'am, that was boy's work. My father and brother planted the corn with a machine."

"A machine?"

"Yes, the horse dragged the machine."

"Did you ride the horse?"

"No, Miss Johnson. Nobody rides horses," Bergit said.

The girls in the back row laughed at this and one of them spoke up, "What about cowboys, Bergit. Haven't you even heard of cowboys?"

"Now be quiet," Miss Johnson said. "Yes, some do ride horses out west and they are cowboys, but probably not on a corn farm where Bergit is from, so don't think you're so smart. There are work horses and there are riding horses."

"Now let's hear from Ethelyn, just a little bit," Miss Johnson said.

I stood up and Miss Johnson gave me the book. I liked to read in my other school. It didn't make me nervous.

First they went to the kitchen where Mammy 'Ria was getting ready to cook the Thanksgiving dinner; then out to the barnyard, where there were two new red calves, and five little puppies belonging to Juno, the dog, for them to see. Then they climbed the barnyard fence and made haste to the pasture where grandfather kept his woolly sheep. "Baa-a!" said the sheep when they saw the children; but then, they always said that, no matter what happened.

There were cows in this pasture, too, and Mary Virginia was afraid of them, even though she knew that they were the mothers of the calves she had seen in the barnyard.

"Silly Mary Virginia!" said John, and Mary Virginia began to cry.

"Don't cry," said Louisa. "Let's go to the hickory-nut tree."

This pleased them all, and they hurried off; but on the way they came to the big shed where grandfather kept his plows and reaper and threshing machine and all his garden tools.

The shed had a long, wide roof, and there was a ladder leaning against it. When John saw that, he thought he must go up on the roof; and then, of course, the twins went, too. Then Louisa and Mary Virginia wanted to go, and although John insisted that girls could not climb, they managed to scramble up the ladder to where the boys were. And there they all sat in a row on the roof.

Miss Johnson stopped me there and said, ""Very good, Ethelyn. Do you like stories?"

"Yes. I guess so."

"Would you like to write a story like this?"

"I don't know. Mama told me not to tell stories."

The older girls laughed again.

"You may sit down, Ethelyn," Miss Johnson said. "Today I want to ask you all to spend your time this evening writing a story like this. Write a story about when you were eight years old, just like the children in this story."

"I don't know when I was eight, Miss Johnson." It was Karen, across the aisle from me. "Nobody knowed how old I was when my mama and daddy died, and I was so little, I don't know either."

"Karen, you can just write me something nice about what you remember from when you were younger."

Miss Johnson then said to the whole class, "You can put aside your sewing tonight, Mrs. McAuliff said so, and bring your story to me when I come back on Thursday, two days from now. You all have your tablets and a pencil. Please write your story neatly on two pages about when you were eight years old."

I picked up my pencil and started writing in the tablet, but Miss Johnson said, "Ethelyn, you can wait until this evening to write, dear."

I put down the pencil and looked around the room, embarrassed. The back row girls were laughing at me this time.

After school and lunch, Mrs. McAuliff took me from the dining room and led me to the same small room where I'd gotten the tablet of paper this morning. A lady nurse in a white dress and cap sat inside.

"Nurse Perlich would like to take a look at you now, Ethelyn. You'll answer her questions and do what she says," and Mrs. McAuliff left.

Nurse Perlich didn't say anything but sat in her chair and stared at me, up and down and around. She got up and raised my chin, felt my neck and looked into my eyes.

She pulled a comb from an apron pocket and began combing through my hair. I hoped she might suggest a haircut.

"You look clean," she said and put the comb away. "Stand up tall now."

I stood up tall. What does she mean, clean? I wash my hair.

"Have you ever been sick?" she asked.

"I had an earache once and a sore throat another time," I told her.

"Was your family sick?"

"My papa got sick and died, the Spanish flu."

Nurse Perlich stepped back a little bit. "When was that?"

"In September, before Mama went away."

"Was your mama sick?"

"She got sick and then she got a baby and went away."

"She got a baby after your father died?"

"I guess so. I don't know really."

"Don't you know where babies come from?"

I was too embarrassed to answer her on this. I kind of knew where babies come from--Mama's stomach.

"Don't you?" Nurse Perlich prodded.

"In our house, wherever they came from, they came two of them after me, but Papa was with us then."

"Yes, well, we will have a talk about that some time soon. Give me your arm now."

She took my hand and pulled my arm toward her. She scraped a kind of pin across the inside of it and it made me squeeze my eyes shut.

"Now we'll listen to your chest. Let me unbutton your dress."

The nurse moved around to the back of me and undid the back buttons. Then she put a cold stethoscope to my chest and moved it all around. She listened through the things in her ears, then straightened herself up.

"We may need to bring you to the infirmary next week. The doctor there will listen to your lungs, like I have, but he's the expert. I'll let you know when. You may go now," and she began writing in a little tablet she had on the desk.

I struggled to button up the back of the dress and went off to the kitchen, as Mrs. McAuliff had told me to, where I was supposed to help slice tomatoes.

That night I sat next to Rosie again in the front room.

"What will you write for Miss Johnson, Rosie?" I asked her.

"I don't know. I don't remember when I was eight. That's so long ago. Do you remember?"

"Yes, I do, because that was when we moved to Minneapolis. That's what I will write about."

I put my tablet on my knees and began to write, trying hard to keep it neat.

"When I was 8," I wrote at the top.

Mama was in the kitchen when I came home from school except she wasn't cooking anything. She sat at the kitchen table with Mr. Jensen. He helped Papa with the boarding house. Papa and Mr. Jensen fixed things and kept the men who lived there from fighting each other.

All the men worked at the railroad yard. Mama cooked for them and did their laundry.

Mr. Jensen was saying how the money was all gone and the railroad wouldn't pay Papa anymore. Then he told Mama he was going to get a different helper and Papa and us would have to go out of the boarding house.

Mama said we could all still do the work for no money if they let us live there.

Mr. Jensen said how he couldn't do that because the railroad wouldn't let women live there no more unless they were married to the manager and Papa couldn't be the manager no more.

Mama told Mr. Jensen how we didn't have any place to go and he said he was sorry and he got up and left so Mama told me to go to my room and wait for my sisters. The next thing I remember is Papa lugging a big trunk down the porch steps and Mama trying to help him but he was mad. He had been mad since Sadie died on the railroad tracks back in the spring. She's my little sister. Sadie was only 5 when she died. Her little grave was by the big church in town. I put spring flowers and dandelions on it sometimes when I walked to school.

Papa was saying to Mama how Minneapolis was big and had lots of work for people to do. He didn't need the railroad or the stockyards no more. He said lots of Norwegians were living in Minneapolis and we would find people there like us who would be nice.

Mama said she would like to go to Brooten where her sister was but Papa yelled he was through with boarding houses where there were too many rough men around his girls.

I remember us standing waiting for the train and Mr. Jensen came up and tried to give Papa some money. Papa said a bad word and didn't take the money so Mr. Jensen went away when the train pulled up. I was excited to be going on a train but when it came in it was so loud I got scared and Mama told me to be a big girl cuz I had seen trains plenty of times but I hadn't rode on any.

Riding on the train I looked out the window until I fell asleep and Pearl shoved me over. Bernie and me and Pearl sat on our bench and Mama and Papa were across from us with the trunk on the floor in front of us. Violet weren't born yet.

The buildings in Minneapolis were so tall and when we got off the train everyone was pushing to get on the train. Papa made us sit on a bench in the train depot and he went to talk to a man at the ticket window. We waited a long time and watched all the people. It was very crowded. We ate some bread Mama pulled out.

When Papa came back from the ticket window we all walked together for a while and Papa had a piece of paper in his hand. Papa and Mama carried the big trunk between them. We stopped at a door and Papa rang a bell.

I stopped because I realized I had already written the two pages Mrs. Johnson wanted. "Oh, dear," I said to myself.

Rosie laughed. I haven't written but two words and look at you? Done already? I got nothing to say."

CHAPTER 8

When Thursday came and school started Miss Johnson asked Bergit to read her story.

Bergit said, "I can't write good," and she held up a piece of paper from her tablet. It wasn't even half full of her writing.

"Just read what you have done, dear. It will be fine."

Bergit stood up and read.

"When I was eight I didn't have a baby in me, but my mama did. My mama died and so did the baby. We kept working on the farm."

She sat down.

"Bergit, thank you for reading. I am sorry your mama died."

Bergit put her head in her arms on the table and Karen, from our bedroom, patted her shoulder a little bit.

"Maybe we need a different story," Miss Johnson said. "Ethelyn?"

I stood up with my tablet and read the two pages I had written on Tuesday night.

"That's very good, Ethelyn, but you didn't tell us what happened. A good story needs a beginning, a middle and an end, doesn't it?"

"Um, I guess so," I said. I held up my tablet. "But I had used up my two papers."

Miss Johnson laughed a little. "Yes, I did say two pages, didn't I? We can get you more paper. Will you write us more? And in another few weeks, we will have you read again?"

I told her I would. It would be exciting and I loved writing. I would much rather do that than the arithmetic problems Mrs. Arnold had given us yesterday.

There is no school on Fridays at the Home School. At this time of year, every girl had to work in the garden all day, out front where I had first seen these girls. It was getting cold and we were put to work picking cucumbers. Some of the girls wore men's jackets that were too big for them. They were like the jacket Papa wore, or the railroad men down in Albert Lea, the ones they wore in the winter. My shawl was fine today, but I realized I didn't have a coat with me. It was left behind when I packed my bags at home, I guess.

Some girls had to pull up the cucumber plants because they were all done and they had to pile the stems over in the back yard. Others hoed down the rows and turned them all into dirt again. I had never worked in a garden, but I remembered Pearl and Bernie hoeing the garden at the railroad house in Albert Lea.

Our ugly dresses got even uglier with the dirt and I was glad tomorrow was Saturday, Wash Day and the day we would get our Sunday dresses to wear for the next day. The other dresses from home were now crumbled up in my one dresser drawer. Rosie said we wouldn't be allowed to wear them anyway, here at school.

"I hate Wash Day," Rosie was saying next to me. We hauled the bushels of cucumbers up to the kitchen side door. "We got to do the sheets and under things and everything. It wears your hands raw. Ladies like us should not have raw hands."

Rosie stuck her nose in the air and pretended to be fanning her face.

I was used to doing wash at home where I pumped water into bins in the side yard and hauled them down to the scary cellar, but Pearl did the hard parts with the heavy wet fabric. The bright laundry room here wouldn't be as bad, but I didn't think all that dirt was ever going to come out of our dresses..

Inside the kitchen where I brought the cucumbers, the three older girls were slicing them and putting them into jars. Steamy vapors from the boiling vinegar made the room warmer than outside and stung my eyes a little.

"Gerty, you wearing that nice watch while getting all dirty. You're just dumb," Dorethea said.

"Shut up, Dorethea," I said to her just as Mrs. Hansen came through the dining room door.

"Shut up, you say?" Mrs. Hansen waggled her big fat finger in my face. "No shut up. That's five points for you!"

I had learned on Thursday all about points because Mrs. McAuliff explained them to all the girls, again, at supper when another new girl had arrived. You get points for picking cucumbers and for washing dishes, two points each. For every bad thing you do, you lose five points. Mrs. McAuliff had said I would get new boots when I had 50 points. This morning I had 12 points, but now I'm back to seven with Mrs. Hansen's announcement. I wasn't good at arithmetic, but it was going to take a long time for me to get new boots for winter. And was I only going to wear my shawl all winter? How could I write to Pearl and ask where my coat was?

"Five points. You put those down and go," Mrs. Hansen shouted at me. "More cucumbers!"

She pushed Rosie and me toward the door, but I managed to stick my tongue out at the older girls as we went.

Breakfast on Saturday morning was tomatoes, cheese and bread, which Mrs. Hansen said was a special treat. I had never eaten cheese for breakfast. "It's because she's German," Rosie said.

After breakfast, Mrs. Hansen took Rosie, Bergit and me into the hot, bright laundry room, where she told us to take off all our clothes, go into the side room, wash ourselves with the rag and warm water, and then to put on the special apron she gave us, like a dress. "After that, we scrub! Rosie will show Ethelyn how."

I was happy to get rid of the dirty dress and took off my watch and the red bow from me hair and put them by the sink Mrs. Hansen said was mine.

"You scrub hard," Mrs. Hansen said as I began to watch what Rosie was doing in the sink next to me. Mrs. Hansen gave me a cake of lye. The dress really didn't get clean, it turned grey. I was slower than the other girls and when I had done a set of sheets and my under things, I emptied the tub out in the yard and returned for my hair ribbon and watch.

They were gone.

The room was empty, but I saw the back of Dorethea's head, with her long black braid, just leaving out the other end. Mrs. Hansen came in the side door, which stopped me from going after Dorethea.

"You done work now. Keep apron on and go outside. Then you play, yes?" and she pointed me out to the back yard.

Rosie was playing jacks by herself just below the kitchen steps. I told her Dorethea had stolen my watch and ribbon. "I'm going to tell Mrs. McAuliff on Monday," I said.

"No, no. You can't do that," Rosie said. "I told on them once and I got 10 points taken away and I never got my book back neither. Mrs. McAuliff said not to tattle."

I sat down on the step then and cried for the first time since my first day of Home School. My watch was the only present from my mother. The doll Mama had made for me went away with Violet, who maybe I would never see again. Would I see anyone again? No one had told me when I might go home, or to Mama, Pearl or Bernie, wherever they were. These girls, these thieves, were my family now.

"Don't cry, Ethy," Rosie said, coming up to sit beside me on the step. "We'll find a way to get those girls and your watch, I promise."

"I don't want to be here, Rosie," I said.

"Me neither, but nobody stays here when they turn 17, so we don't have that long to wait, as long as we don't have babies." Rosie started giggling. "I don't know how we could ever do that since we don't have no boys here."

Rosie's giggling made me giggle, too. Boys. I knew you had to have a boy to have a baby and at least I didn't have that problem. But then I thought about Violet, who was kind of like my baby, and I started crying again.

"I want Violet," I told Rosie.

"Your little sister? Don't be sad. Maybe she'll go to a nice rich family here in Minneapolis and you will get to go live with them, like Karen's going to do soon."

"I don't want to live with another family," I said.

Just then the back door burst open and Mr. Hansen, the gardener, came out.

"Baseball, girls, you want to play?"

He shot out the door so fast we had to get up quick and get out of his way.

"We go over to field," he said. "Come!"

I looked at Rosie, hoping she would explain. Rosie was all smiles.

"Come on, Ethelyn, I told you. Time to learn to catch!" She pulled me up from the step.

For being married to fat Mrs. Hansen, Mr. Hansen was sure skinny and fast. We had to run to catch up and he had already gathered other girls who had been standing around in the field where the cows usually grazed. The cows were in their barn now. The girls clapped when Mr. Hansen came over carrying a baseball bat and a ball.

When the girls reached a water trough in the field he stopped and put his equipment on the grass, which was turning brown now that fall was here.

"This may be our last chance, girls," he said. "We practice for spring before snow comes now."

"Sarah, you pitch." He tossed a big ball at Sarah, who caught it like she was expecting it all along. Sarah was tall and looked a lot like a boy. She had a boy haircut. "Sarah, you throw ball for new girl, Ett-lyn, to catch."

Sarah stepped back farther from us and pointed to where Ethelyn should stand.

68

"Ready?" she said.

I stood there.

"Ready," I said, though I wasn't sure I was.

"No, no." Mr. Hansen came over to stand beside me. He bent his knees a little and held his hands in front of him, showing me.

"No. Like this. So. This way you ready."

I tried to stand the way he did. The other girls stood by and watched.

"I'll go real slow," Sarah said as she prepared to throw to me. She threw the ball underhand. It came right toward me, but I leaned too far forward and nearly fell over trying to grab it. I missed the ball.

"You move feet to go to ball," Mr. Hansen said, and he picked the ball from the grass and threw it back to Sarah.

"That was my fault," Sarah said. "I didn't throw far enough. Just watch."

As the ball came more slowly to me this time, I could tell just where to stand to grab it and I caught it using both hands. Ouch. It hurt, but I quick pushed it into my chest so I wouldn't lose it.

"Gut. Gut. Zehr gut," Mr. Hansen said.

"You two play," he said, and he pulled another ball from his jacket pocket, picked up the bat and took the other girls further out into the field. I saw him hit one ball out to them and they all ran up to try to catch it. Mr. Hansen hit another and another.

"Come on, Ethelyn," Sarah said. "You've got to practice if you're going to be on the team in spring."

She got ready to pitch to me. When she did, I ran up just a little and caught it in both hands, without using my chest. We did this many more times, until it was getting dark and the bell rang to tell us it was time for supper.

"You good catch," Mr. Hansen said as we all walked toward the back door. "Next week, we play a real game on a team."

I didn't know what being on a team and playing a game could be like, but suddenly I couldn't wait for the second week of school and housework to be over with so Saturday would come quicker.

CHAPTER 9

At breakfast on Sunday morning, a fancy dressed lady named Mrs. Wiborg joined us girls. When everyone was done eating, she stood and said, "Protestants?" and called a list of names that included mine and Rosie's.

We wore our Sunday dresses that Mrs. Hansen had delivered to our pegs last night, all shaped like the school day ones, but of a material not quite as rough as those. Mine was very plain, a solid navy blue. I hated navy blue. The Protestants followed Mrs. Wiborg out the front door and down the sidewalk to the church whose bells rang every hour, night and day. I heard them when I was awake sometimes.

Rosie and I walked side by side and Rosie whispered that all the other school girls who did not stand up when Mrs. Wiborg called for Protestants were Catholics, and they weren't allowed to go to their own church because they had been bad. A nun would come to the school, she said, and recite lessons with them this morning. And all the ones having babies, they didn't even get to hear the lessons.

"You know the very best thing about playing baseball?" Rosie whispered.

"No, what?" I asked.

"That mean, pregnant Dorethea can't play with us."

Us two had to stop giggling because we had reached the church steps.

Mrs. Wiborg put her fingers to her lips and held the heavy wooden church door open for us. We filed into the pews she showed us near the back. The 12 of us took up two pews altogether.

In other pews, gray-haired ladies with lace collars turned to smile at us. One had reached out to touch my hand across the aisle, saying, "Welcome, dear."

Church was a lot of standing up and sitting down and standing up again, just like I remembered from the church where confirmation happened. It was not much different than that church, but I couldn't be sure. We had gone only a little. Mama liked church, but Papa never went with us.

In the recitation of the Apostle's Creed, everyone used the book, but I could still remember it from confirmation classes and I said it without looking. Finally, the pastor got up in a big wooden box at the front. I tried hard to pay attention, even though Rosie sitting next to me had brought along yarn and was trying to get me to do Cat's Cradle as the pastor spoke.

"God's love is for everyone," the pastor said. "That's what Christ's presence with us, and his resurrection, are meant to teach us, first and foremost."

I liked the word "foremost" and wished I had my pencil and paper to write it down. Next I heard him say, "We are the products of his amazing grace. So many have died. Our men-our boys-are dying overseas and dying down the street. What have we done to deserve this, you may be asking. Is God angry with us? We have won the war, but they are still dying. How come he is angry with us?"

Did we win the war, I wondered. Nobody had told me this. Pearl said back at home that it was ending and I had asked how she knew. She just said it was coming to an end soon. Everybody said so. I didn't remember much before the war, except that people seemed a lot happier then. Not so strict.

"God wants you to care for the sick, though you may die yourself," the pastor was saying. "The sick are everywhere today. The Spanish flu still torments us."

The ladies across the aisle nodded at this, as the pastor read off a list of names. "We pray for the departed souls of our congregation--Lloyd Johnson, Torvald Ingebretsen, Floyd Halvorson, Al Swenson, Lyle Willey, Leonard Wiborg and, just last week, little Lester Holte."

Wiborg? Was that Mrs. Wiborg's husband, I wondered. I noticed some of the ladies across the aisle were dabbing at their eyes, wiping their noses, but Mrs. Wiborg sat with a small smile on her face.

"God wants you to give money to the war effort, though you may be poor. It is the way we show love to those who remain. Love the children. The children." And as he paused he looked in the direction of the girls' pew, as did several heads of the old ladies.

"The children are in trouble. Let the children come unto us," he said and then got down slowly from his box. A bunch of ladies in red robes stood up and began to sing.

While the ladies sang, a man passed the offering plate. When it came to the girls' pews, Mrs. Wiborg stood up and leaned into the aisle to place money in the pan, smiling at everyone around her as she did so. The man holding it winked at us girls and kept walking.

As we all followed Mrs. Wiborg out, the pastor stood at the sidewalk greeting everyone. He patted each girl's hand as she passed and said, "My child."

I wasn't sure if I should speak to him or say thank you or say anything. When we had gone to church with Mama, all of us passed by the pastor quickly and didn't speak to him, and neither did Mama. I thought that's what I should do.

Walking back to the house, Mrs. Wiborg stepped beside me and said, "You should say good morning to the pastor, Ethelyn. It's the polite thing to do."

"I'm sorry," I said, and I really was. I had not done the right thing in front of the pastor.

"No need to be sorry, dear. Just do better next time," Mrs. Wiborg said.

CHAPTER 10

My first Sunday dinner at Home School was sliced potatoes with a few bits of ham in them. Afterwards, we all went to the front room with Mrs. Wiborg and she announced she was staying the afternoon to teach anyone who wanted to learn how to sew.

I was the first to step over to her. "I would like to sew a new dress for church," I said.

Mrs. Wiborg laughed and said, "That's very good of you, Ethelyn, but with the war, material is hard to come by and is very expensive, as you may know. With all the boys coming back now, things will be even tighter for a while."

She said I would have to earn many points to make a dress, but I could do it if I worked very hard here. "Will you, Ethelyn? Will you work hard?"

"I'll try," I said, though I didn't really see how it would be possible. I had to earn new boots first. And then maybe a winter coat. A dress would have to wait, even if I could earn some material.

"Let's get you sewing first. Then we'll see," Mrs. Wiborg said.

She sat beside me and took a piece of square, beige cloth in her hands. She then threaded a needle like I'd seen Pearl do a thousand times. She held the cloth toward me and sewed a few stitches. Then she handed it to me to try.

"In, down, over, up, out. You see?'

I made three wobbly stitches and then stuck myself in the finger.

"Slowly," Mrs. Wiborg said. "You need to have patience. Keep trying. See if you can do 10 straight now."

"Mrs. Wiborg," I said. "Did your husband die in the war?"

"Yes, dear. The very first month of it, which seems a long time ago now, doesn't it? We all must get on with life, don't we?"

She moved away to help some of the other girls. By the end of the afternoon, I had sewn many crooked lines across the cloth, and exactly one straight line along its shortest side. Mrs. Wiborg said it was very good. "You are ready to try a hem. I'll teach you that next week. With more practice you will be good at fine work. You have even stitches," she said. "We must get you a thimble. I will bring one next week and a basket of your own."

Maybe I just had learned a thing or two watching Pearl sew all those years.

"Thank you, Mrs. Wiborg, and I'm sorry to hear about your husband." I didn't know if that was the right thing to say, but she patted my hand and said, "You're very kind."

Dorethea was at the top of the stairs when I went up that night. "Church lady," she said with a sneer on her face, standing in front of our bedroom door. "You're a stupid church lady."

"I am not," I said, though I didn't know it was a bad thing to be a church lady.

"You're Mrs. Wiborg's pet now," Dorethea said. "Teacher's pet."

I suddenly remembered how Dorethea had stolen my watch yesterday and my ears got hot, my heart pounding.

"At least I am not a thief," I said, and I shoved Dorethea against our bedroom door. She shoved me back against the opposite wall. Rosie, who had come up the steps behind me, quick stepped in and stomped on Dorethea's foot.

"Meanie!" Rosie hollered into Dorthea's face.

Dorethea slapped Rosie. With my face growing hot, I heaved myself forward from the wall and stomped on Dorethea's other foot just as Mrs. Hansen came up the stairs with a basket of linens.

"Girls! Bad girls!" she said. She put her big body and the basket between the three of us. "I take points! Big points! Go to rooms!"

More points gone. My winter boots and coat, not to mention a church dress, slipped further away.

Bergit was all excited and wanted to talk about Dorethea while we were in bed again, but I told her I had to write a letter right then and there.

Dear Pearl and Bernie,

I don't know how I'll get this letter to you, but I will. I just wanted to tell you what kind of school you and Aunt Hattie sent me to. I live with a bunch of mean pregnant girls and thieves here. I hope you're happy. They make us pick cucumbers and wash our own ugly dresses. I bet it's nicer where you are and you're getting paid a lot of money to do the work you do. Me, I get nothing but points taken away and I don't even have decent boots. I just think you should know this in case Aunt Sigrid says she could use another helper.

Ethelyn (NOT Gerty!)

CHAPTER 11

Exactly a week after I arrived at Home School, I was called to Nurse Perlich's office again. This time I knew the way and found the nurse in her tiny exam room.

"Ethelyn, come in. Are you feeling well?"

"Yes. I feel fine."

"Remember I said you may have to visit the infirmary? It is all arranged now. We are going together on Wednesday. You will see a doctor."

"Why? Am I sick?"

"Your lungs don't sound right somehow. I'm sure you are fine, but it is best we have the doctor look at you," she said. "He told me that you should be isolated, so tonight and tomorrow you will sleep in the other building in back. Mrs. Hansen will bring you food on a tray, and some of your things. That's tonight and all day tomorrow now. We can't have you making the other girls sick."

"But I don't feel sick."

"I know, but this is best."

She led me out the school's back door, crossing to the right of the field where they had played baseball, to a small barn. Mr. and Mrs. Hansen, I now knew, lived at the top of this building, but Nurse Perlich led me into the lower level through a side door.

Just inside the floor was cluttered with hoes, rakes and baskets filled with just picked squash and cucumbers. She led me to the back where a room had been made by hanging sheets from the ceiling. Inside the sheets was a cot even smaller than the one in my bedroom with the other girls. The one solid wall was lined with hay bales from floor to ceiling. A wash basin on a wooden stand stood next to the cot. A small window above the hay bales above the cot was too high to even look through.

"You sit on the bed and I will take your temperature," Nurse Perlich said.

"You are fine. See. Nothing to worry about," she said after examining the thermometer. "I will get Mrs. Hansen to bring you a book and your tablet. Okay now."

After she left, I sat at the head of the bed and noticed how cold it was, but stuffy, too. The blanket was very thin. I should have asked for another blanket. I was glad I had put on my wool stockings this morning. An oil lamp stood by the washbasin, but I noticed there were no matches. It was gloomy and damp and very lonely.

I thought maybe I was going to die like Papa. They were saying the sickness was getting done with now, just like the war, but maybe I got it by taking Papa's hand that day when he died. I looked under my stockings to see if I was turning purple. I wasn't. I wish there was a mirror so I could see my face. I poked at my throat to see if anything hurt. It didn't.

I remembered going to see a doctor only once, back in Albert Lea when I got that sore throat. Mama had sent me another time to get medicine for Bernie at the doctor's office just up on Main Street. Mama was the one who had doctored me and my sisters. I wondered what an infirmary in the city looks like.

I lay quietly on the bed listening to my breathing. It sounded normal to me. The church bell rang five times and then Mrs. Hansen came in. She wore a mask over her mouth and nose and so her voice was muffled.

"Your dinner, a book, papier and pencil. Now eat."

79

She set the tray with these things on the foot of the bed and went away quickly.

I ate the bread and the small piece of bologna Mrs. Hansen had left, and I drank some water. There was no milk. Mrs. Hansen left in such a hurry I didn't have a chance to ask her for matches to light the lamp, or another blanket.

It got dark early now and the little room of sheets was very dark by the time the church bell struck seven times. I couldn't see my fingers in front of me to do the Cat's Cradle with the piece of yarn I had found in my pocket. The game didn't work well without a second person anyway.

Soon I heard Mr. and Mrs. Hansen's footsteps and their talking as they headed up to their room above my head. They would not come down again tonight, most likely. I got up, took the blanket off the bed, got the tablet and pencil, and went outside to sit on the step of the little building. The moon was just bright enough to see, so I decided to finish the story I was writing for Miss Johnson, who had said she wanted to hear the end.

At the front of the big dark building where Papa stopped a fat lady opened the door. Papa said to her that he was looking for Lars.

Who Lars? The lady said. We have three of them. Papa then spoke a long time to her in fast Norwegian I didn't understand. The lady said Lars is on three. You walk up but I must have money if you stay.

Papa gave her some money and he and Mama lifted the big trunk up many steps, stopping a lot to rest. They would not let Pearl or Bernie or me try to help.

When we got to the third floor Papa knocked on a door and when it opened he spoke Norwegian to the man inside.

Papa moved the trunk inside which was only one room and a sink behind a dirty curtain in the corner.

The man said we were welcome. He was nice.

Lars said to Papa that tomorrow there would be work and when there was work Papa could find us our own room.

We all slept on blankets on the floor of this man's room and it was very crowded. The man had a bed in the corner behind another curtain that he shut and slept there.

Papa and Lars left early in the morning and told Mama to make coffee. She went to the trunk for bread but there was only a little bit. When we were done drinking coffee Mama said we would walk down the street. We walked two blocks and came to a building with a red cross on it. Mama took us inside and a lady who was wearing a uniform like a soldier 's spoke Norwegian to Mama and took us to a table and gave us milk and more bread.

The lady said to Mama you will meet Mrs. Jordahl soon. She will have rooms if your husband gets money.

In the other side of the room there were four men who were very old and they spat snoose into a coffee can like Papa's papa did back in Albert Lea before he died. It smelled bad in the room.

I heard the door open above me on the steps. Mr. Hansen was coming down with a lantern. I quick got back into my room, but I had to stand inside the door for a few minutes before I could see my way to the bed.

I spent all day Tuesday inside my dreary sheet room and wondered what Rosie was doing and if anybody had told her where I had gone. When I heard Mr. and Mrs. Hansen talking as they went to the big house in the morning, I got up to look out the small window in the door. I could only see the chickens in the yard and the back door to the house, but I stood on a crate watching until I saw Mrs. Hanson come out carrying a tray and wearing her mask again. I scrambled back behind the sheets and into the bed.

"Wacht Auf!" Mrs. Hansen muffled voice came at the door. She barely came inside the sheets and set the tray down.

"Please, Mrs. Hansen, I would like to light the lamp."

"One match I give you. Oil is expensive. You wait til night."

She tossed a match onto the bed.

"Thank you," I said, but Mrs. Hansen was nearly out the door already.

I nibbled at the breakfast, bread and rhubarb jam and cold coffee, but I did not feel much like eating. I read the book Mrs. Hansen had left yesterday. It was a child's book of fairy tales that I might have read in school already, but it had pictures and rhyming words, which were fun to say out loud over and over until I got tired of it.

I was asleep when Mrs. Hansen returned with lunch on another tray. I looked at it, but fell back to sleep. I slept until nearly time for supper.

"You no eat?" Mrs. Hansen said. "Ach. You won't get well if no eat."

She took the lunch tray and left another. I was not hungry in my dark little room. I had the shivers now, but my head felt hot. My chest had a dull pain on one side. It hurt when I breathed in.

When I heard the church bell ring, I wanted to sit up to see if the pain would go away, so I lit the lamp by the bed and started writing my story again.

After two more nights on the floor in Mr. Lars room Papa came to the room and said we were moving now to Mrs. Jordahl's house.

That's where we still live below Mrs. Jordahl and next door to another big family where my friend Kjersti lived.

That's all I found in my notebook the next morning. I must have fallen asleep again.

The lantern! It had gone out.

Nurse Perlich came in and heard me when I said, "Oh, dear" about the lamp. She did not wear a mask.

"Goodness, dear, you have used up the lantern oil. Come now."

I had slept two nights in my dress and it was quite wrinkled. When I stood up to smooth it down, the nurse said, "We've no time for that now," and she pulled a brush through my hair so quickly it hurt. "We'll be going. We have a short walk."

We walked in the opposite direction from the church, past the big ball field I had seen on my first day and forgotten about. It felt like we walked a very long way. I was tired and my feet had begun to ache in my boots without heels. My shoulders were aching, too, and my chest. I was cold and it was a very bright, sunny day.

We were in a new neighborhood now, with huge, dark stone houses all around. Each had names above their big porches. Blaisdale Place. Women's Club. Franklin Infirmary. We turned in at the last one.

A lady greeted us at the desk inside the door. "The doctor's expecting you, Nurse Perlich. Go on in."

We went into a room that was just big enough to hold a tall table with a white sheet on it and one white cabinet with shiny tools inside. A man with a mustache and a white coat sat on a high stool writing something.

"Nurse Perlich, is this your patient?"

"Yes, doctor. Ethelyn, this is Dr. Vanesek. He'll look at you now."

"How do you feel, Ethelyn?" he said.

"I'm tired from walking."

"Oh, are you now, a big girl like you?"

He felt all around my throat, then he looked into my ears. Like Nurse Perlich had done, he listened to my chest with a stethoscope, stopping a long time to listen each time he moved it to a new spot, front and back.

"Sit still now," he said once. "Breath in."

He pulled the stethoscope from his ears finally, saying to Nurse Perlich. "It's a mild case, to be sure, but with the sickness all around us, she should go to the sanatorium. She'll beat it more quickly there."

"Yes, doctor. I will make the arrangements immediately."

"To be safe, we'll keep her here while you retrieve her things. They've issued orders now. No sick people on streetcars."

84

"Yes, doctor," and she helped me off the table.

Nurse Perlich took me into another room where there were two cots like the one behind my sheet room in the barn. A girl was in the cot furthest from the door.

"You lie here and rest, Ethelyn, and I'll be back before you know it."

"Do I have the sickness? The Spanish flu?" I pictured Papa and his purple face.

"Heavens no," Nurse Perlich said. "You have tuberculosis."

Tuberculosis? I tried saying the word right. I had heard it before. Was it better or worse than the Spanish flu?

"But can't I go home? I mean, to the school?" I said, as the nurse fluffed my pillow.

"Not for a while, dear. Other people can now make you very sick. The sanitarium will get you well, it will just be a while."

Mrs. Perlich left me and I looked over at the girl who had been watching us from the other bed.

"Hello," the girl said to me in a whispering voice.

"Do you have tuberculosis?" I asked.

"No. Scarlet fever. I'm going to the hospital soon." The girl closed her eyes.

The hospital. Somehow that sounded better to me than a sanatorium. I fell asleep, but in a few minutes my own coughing woke me up.

Nurse Perlich had to wake me up, though, when she returned. She shook me a little and explained how we must take a short streetcar ride across the city. She said we both had to wear masks and she put one over my mouth and nose.

85

"It's important not to cough on anyone, dear." She made me put on one of the ugly men's coats the school girls wore on cold days.

The steps up onto the streetcar seemed awfully high and when Nurse Perlich sat me on a bench next to an older lady, the lady got up and asked the driver to let her out. All the windows in the streetcar were open and I was cold to the bone, leaning against Nurse Perlich now.

The county sanitarium was one wing of General Hospital, a name I read etched above the door. I was put into a large room with six other cots, all occupied by girls about my age and a few ladies, but all of them were asleep. I wanted to sleep, too. I had fallen asleep on the short, cold streetcar ride. Nurse Perlich told me she would check on me once each week, on Wednesdays, and that she would write to my sisters.

"Can you ask them to send me a winter coat?" I managed to ask.

"I'll put in in the letter, but no promises."

I thought about asking Nurse Perlich to write Mama, too, but I was too tired to say it. I thought about how I wasn't going to get my next sewing lesson, a hem, from Mrs. Wiborg on Sunday. Or the thimble and basket she had been promised. And when would I get to read Miss Johnson the ending of my story?

They tell me I slept most of two weeks, though the room bustled with activity--the clatter of carts to the bedsides and the nurses talking with each other. The medicines they gave me made me sleepy and I had strange dreams about Sadie and Papa. In the daylight hours I was always groggy except when my coughing attacks happened.

One night I was startled awake with loud voices out in the hallway, women and men, and wondered what the trouble was. A fire, I thought? I couldn't hear clearly through the room's heavy doors. A great bell, which I had heard on Sundays, clanged somewhere outside the window at the opposite end of the big room. None of the other girls in their cots appeared to stir, but I got myself up and listened at the doors. I jumped back when the door swung open from someone pushing in from the hallway.

"The war is over. Over for good," the voices outside were shouting. Just as I stepped into the hall, I was lifted up by a man dressed all in white, who twirled me in his arms and gave me a wet kiss on my cheek. He made me dizzy. A laughing nurse grabbed me from the man and led me back to my bed where I fell back to sleep amid the noise.

"Was it a dream, nurse?" I asked the lady who brought my breakfast tray in the morning.

"What dear?"

"The war?"

"No, not a dream! Isn't it grand? Our boys will come home now. We are all safe."

I barely remembered a time without the war. I was only 12 when it had begun, with Papa telling us all at the supper table that his brother, Uncle Arthur, would go off to fight. As I ate my breakfast, I thought how happy Mama will be, but it made me sad that Papa did not live to hear this good news. Then I had a happy thought that maybe now Pearl and Bernie would find boys among the returning soldiers and they would have husbands.

In another few days Nurse Perlich arrived at my bed and said it was the day before Thanksgiving. I had lost track of the days in my sleepiness.

"Goodness, you're awake for once! And you have good color," she said.

"It's Wednesday already?" I asked.

"Yes, the first one I've seen you awake. You are indeed looking better," the nurse said. "You didn't even say hello last time I was here."

The nurse handed me a letter and told me to see if I could sit up to read it.

"I can sit up," I said and the nurse pulled the pillows up behind me.

Dear Ethelyn-

We are very sorry to hear you are sick. We cannot come visit you now, because our work is very busy. This is when the loggers prepare to start chopping trees as soon as the ground freezes. Aunt Hattie has written us to say that Violet is well and that Mama will stay in bed until the baby comes in February. I am making you a winter coat to have for Christmas.

Your sister,
Pearl

"Isn't that nice," Nurse Perlich said. "A new coat for Christmas."

"But she didn't write anything about me coming up there. And I want to see Violet."

"I don't know about that dear, but the doctor says you're doing splendidly. Most people with t.b. are sick a very long time, but you're clearly on the road to recovery. You may just get to come home to us at Christmas time, you wait and see. I'll be back to check on you again next Wednesday."

Now that I felt less sleepy, I spent my days in bed reading books. A Ladies Aid group wheeled in a cart every few days and let all of us who could sit up pick whichever book we wanted from it. Yesterday I handed back the two childish books I had finished and picked out a really thick one from the cart. It was called, "The Tin Woodman of Oz."

"That will keep you busy enough," the lady said as she handed me the book. "You're very brave to pick such a big one."

The other sick girls were mostly asleep, though, so reading was the only way I could pass the time and it made me feel a little less lonely.

On Thanksgiving, I had a turkey dinner in bed, I ate everything but the peas, and then someone gave me a turkey hat to wear for the occasion. It was babyish, but I felt so well that I didn't care.

In another two weeks, the sanitarium nurses led me into a nearby sunroom for an hour a day. I liked to lay on a chaise in there to feel the sun when it peeked through. In two weeks, I wasn't even half done with "The Tin Man," because I would read and re-read every chapter. I loved the adventures the characters were having in a strange land, but I always wanted to know if Dorothy's family was looking for her.

When Nurse Perlich returned the next Wednesday, she found me sitting on a bench in the sunroom letting the sun hit my face. I had blankets covering my legs.

"Goodness, Ethelyn, aren't you the healthy one? And, now we know the reason why."

"Why?" I asked.

"Dr. Vanasek thinks you don't have t.b. at all, but you had pneumonia. He could see it on that x-ray picture they took of you here last week. Because you're so strong, you fought it off, so there's a blessing. Most people die of pneumonia. He says you will be home to the school before Christmas."

Home, I thought. But how strange to think of Home School as home. I really had only lived there two weeks, but it was the only home I had to go home to now.

CHAPTER 12

When Nurse Perlich brought me back to Home School, it was December 16 and the big house was bustling to get ready for a Christmas party. Rosie met us at the door and squealed, grasping my hands and jumping up and down.

"Now, we must keep Ethelyn quiet another week or so. No excitement," the nurse scolded Rosie.

While the other girls went to school and worked in the kitchen, I had to stay in bed, but I just kept on reading. The book cart lady at the sanitarium let me take "The Tin Man" with me when I left because, the lady had said, I deserved to know how the story ended.

One evening as I was reading, someone knocked on my door and I hoped it was Rosie. But it turns out it was a lady I didn't know. She came in and asked if she could sit at the foot of my bed.

"I'm Mrs. Waite dear," the lady said, "I'm here to help you write a letter to your mama and one to your sisters. All the girls downstairs are doing that right now, too. I have this pretty stationery and Christmas cards for you to sign. Then we'll get them right into the mail."

I didn't see why I needed this lady to write for me since I could write perfectly well, but maybe I wasn't allowed because the paper was so pretty, so I agreed.

"Will you just write what I say?" I asked.

"Yes, dear. Go ahead," she said, holding a fancy fountain pen over her paper. "Let's start with your mama first."

"Dear Mama and Violet," I began. "I don't have t.b. anymore and never did. I had pneumonia, but I am fine now. The nurse says I could have died but I was too strong."

Mrs. Waite interrupted me. "Dear, maybe for a Christmas letter, we should tell only the happy stories. What do you say?"

I didn't like this one bit. I thought this was a happy story. I didn't die, did I?

"Okay." I started over.

"Here at school I have a friend named Rosie and I learned to catch a baseball before I got sick. In the spring, we will have a baseball team unless you ask me to come to stay with you, which I would like very much. I miss you and Violet and of course I want to meet the new baby when it comes.

Please write to me, or tell Aunt Hattie to write to me if you can't, and tell me about your Christmas. Your daughter, Ethelyn."

"That's very good, Ethelyn. Now, you sign your name here on the card and I will see it gets mailed tomorrow. Now, your sisters, yes?"

I thought for a few moments to think what to say.

"Are you the wife of Judge Waite?" I asked the woman, suddenly realizing this must be the wife the judge had mentioned when he signed my papers two months ago.

"Yes, he is my husband," Mrs. Waite said. "He wishes he would have had occasion to come by here himself, but things have been so busy lately."

"Don't you think he's mean, taking all us girls away from our families?" I couldn't help it. That mean old judge could do anything he wanted, couldn't he?

"It's the law, Ethelyn. He's just doing his job to make sure you girls are taken care of."

"I was being taken care of just fine before he signed those papers."

Her pen was still poised above the blank piece of stationery and she had stopped smiling. "Go ahead, dear. Let's finish your letter to your sisters."

I gave her a good stare, then began.

"Dear Bernie & Pearl," I said. "Thank you for writing me a letter when I was sick. I am better now and back at the school you sent me to. I have a friend named Rosie. I hope you like your work and you are not sad. I do need a winter coat because I have not earned any points while I was sick. If you ever want me to come work with you, I will. Please tell Aunt Sigrid. Your sister, Ethelyn."

"Now dear, do you think they could really send you a winter coat?"

"Pearl said in a letter at Thanksgiving that she was making me one. She's a good seamstress, which I will be when I get well."

"Certainly, dear. I also wanted to tell you that we are having a party here, the Ladies Guild, on Christmas Eve, so you must get rest and take care of yourself and be all better by that time. Can you do that?"

"I can take care of myself," I told her.

On the Monday before Christmas Eve, I had to go have another check-up with Dr. Vanesek. He listened to my chest again and said I was cured. He told me to stay quiet in bed for three more days, but after that I could get up if I promised to rest for one hour each day. I was so thrilled and so was Rosie when I told her the news.

Rosie and I spent Christmas Eve day with all the other girls cutting out stars and angels from colored paper Miss Johnson, the reading teacher, had left with the girls in their last class before Christmas vacation. Miss Johnson wouldn't be back until January. We made paper chains for the tree and put them aside for when the Ladies Guild came later in the day.

Dorethea was no longer with the older group of girls and sharing my bedroom. While I was at the sanitarium, she had had her baby.

"We didn't have a going away party for her or nothing," Rosie had told me first thing. "That's just not fair. I don't care about Dorethea, but at least we could have had a welcome to this world party for the baby, don't you think?"

We sat at a little table set up special in the front room and Mrs. Hansen bustled in and out with cookies on platters and filling a punch bowl with Christmas cider.

Rosie slipped a small wrapped package out of her apron pocket and gave it to me.

"What's this?" I cried, turning over the small package. "I didn't make you anything."

"Open it," Rosie said.

Inside I found my watch from Mama!

"What? Oh, Rosie, how did you..!"

"When Dorethea left to have her baby, I quick snuck into her room, your room, and looked in all the drawers. It was there all along," Rosie said.

"Oh, thank you, you little sneak." I turned it over to read the inscription on the back again. "To Ethelyn, from Mother."

Then I told Rosie how I hadn't received a Christmas letter back from Mama or Pearl, so I guessed that meant Pearl wasn't going to make that winter coat she had promised. "Nurse Perlich gave me one of those men's coats, but it's even worse than these stupid dresses."

The Christmas party, when the Ladies Guild arrived, got loud very quickly with so many women and so many girls in our sitting room. Plus the women had brought a man with them who had very quickly set up a Christmas tree in the corner. It took up quite a few chair spaces. We all ate Mrs. Hansen's cookies and some of the women brought cakes and pies and a Julekake like I remembered Mama had made once for Christmas before the war.

After we girls and all the women worked together to decorate the tree, I felt kind of sick from all the cookies and cakes. With the tree ready we all sang "Silent Night" out of little books the ladies had brought. Then the ladies made us girls sit quietly while our names were called out one by one. Each girl went to the Christmas tree and got a wrapped present from one of the ladies.

Rosie was ahead of me and she came back to show what was in her package, a pair of stockings and a cross-stitch pattern to sew. Other girls got fancy aprons and new hair ribbons.

When it was my turn, far down on the list because I was "Thompson," my package seemed much bigger than the ones the other girls had received.

"Ethelyn, they tell us you were very sick and couldn't earn your points for a long time, so we got you what we knew you needed most," Mrs. Wiborg explained.

I sat down and tore the wrapping off the package, saving the ribbon in my pocket. It was a ladies black cloth coat, warm enough for winter and good enough for church.

"Thank you," I said. It made me happy, but I wondered if this somehow meant they all knew Pearl was never going to send me the handmade coat she had promised. Then I noticed Mrs. Waite, who had helped me write the letters, smiling especially at me and I figured she must have arranged for the coat. It fit me perfectly, though it had a little moth hole in the middle of the back and one of the hems of a sleeve was coming loose.

After Christmas, we didn't have school, but were set to work during the day cleaning the big house from top to bottom. "Early spring cleaning," Mrs. Hansen called it, but we all knew she was just trying to keep us busy and out of trouble.

I had several more sewing lessons on Sundays and I learned to make a hem with Mrs. Wiborg that first Sunday after Christmas. My next lesson was to repair stockings like Rosie could already do. Mrs. Wiborg said I had to make up for the time lost when I was at the sanitarium. She brought me the promised thimble and a little sewing basket of my own.

Without school, the cleaning and laundry were done in the mornings and we were then allowed to do as we wanted in the afternoons and evenings, as long as we stayed out of Mrs. Hansen's way. I tried to concentrate on my sewing or reading the big book from the sanitarium if Rosie didn't get me into playing a game. Rosie once rounded up four girls in the sitting room and got them all to play catch with a ball of yarn, but Mrs. Hansen quickly put a stop to that.

CHAPTER 13

It was four days into the New Year and nobody had mentioned anything about my birthday, January 6. I wondered if Mrs. McAuliff or Mrs. Hansen or any one even knew that. At home my birthday got kind of jumbled up with all the Christmas activities, but Mama always made sure to do a little something special on "Little Christmas" which was Epiphany, the same date as my birthday. Other girls at the home school had had small birthday parties, but no one had ever asked me when my birthday was.

On January 6, I had lived at the home school exactly three months, if you counted the sanitarium days. After breakfast that day, Mrs. McAuliff said she had to take me to visit Judge Waite again right that day, an idea I didn't like at all. Would the judge send me away from Home School to be somebody's maid? Maybe he would say I could now go to Mama? I worried, but at least liked the idea of wearing my new winter coat outdoors for the first time. Mrs. McAuliff said she guessed it was below zero outside, so I really needed it.

Riding the streetcar with Mrs. MacAuliff, I twirled my watch around and around on my wrist. I was too nervous to ask Mrs. McAuliff what the judge might say.

"Your honor, we have Ethelyn here today for a renewal."

"Ethelyn, I am sorry I have not been to the school to see you. Mrs. McAuliff keeps me too busy."

"Yes, your honor," I said without Mrs. McAuliff telling me to.

"I understand you were quite sick for a time?"

97

"Yes, your honor. I am fine now, thank you," I said.

"That is good to hear. Good to hear. Mrs. McAuliff?"

"Your honor, we have had no communication from Ethelyn's family--her mother, or aunts or sisters--except one note to Ethelyn that did not indicate any change in their circumstances. I request that Ethelyn's time with us continue another three months until we can better ascertain the family's current plans."

"That sounds reasonable enough to me," the judge said. "So granted."

He gave Mrs. McAuliff a piece of paper.

I waited until we were safely out on the street before I asked Mrs. McAuliff, "Three months more?"

"Yes, Ethelyn, you really haven't been with us long enough to learn a trade. With your illness and without word from your family, it appears this can't be helped. You are not of age yet. Only sixteen."

I just stared out the streetcar windows the rest of the ride back. When we came in the Home School door, Mrs. Hansen met us with a package in her hands.

"This come for you," she said as she handed it to me.

I could see right away it wasn't large enough to be the long-promised coat from Pearl, but I got excited just the same.

"You may open it, dear," Mrs. McAuliff said, but her face looked worried.

I sat and saw that "Albert Lea" was written on the return address. Mama! I thought. A birthday present?

I felt through the paper inside and found something hard and square. I pulled the paper away to find a formal portrait of Mama, the one that had hung in her bedroom with Papa. Papa had the photo made for Mama on one of her birthdays.

Then I found a note written on rough brown paper, unfolded it and read it to myself:

Ethelyn,

I'm sorry but your Mama died because the baby came too early and your mama was not strong. The baby lived, so we must be grateful for that. I have visited Violet in her home with other youngsters and she is talking now. Your Mama said to give you this picture.

Aunt Hattie

I dropped the things in my lap and cried.

"What is it, dear?" Mrs. McAuliff said.

She took the letter from my hand and read it out loud to Mrs. Hansen.

"Oh, schade. Zehr schade. Too bad," Mrs. Hansen said. "Good you are here with us now. An orphan."

"You may go to your room now, Ethelyn. No chores for you today. I am sorry about your mother," Mrs. MacAuliff said.

Up in my room, I looked at Mama's picture a long time and cried until I fell asleep. The first thing when I woke up it was dark and I remembered the awful news and cried some more. Then I got another thought. I now had another baby sister, or was it a brother, in Albert Lea. It was still my birthday, too. Not a "little Christmas" type of gift from Mama at all. I sobbed.

Mrs. Hansen came up to my room just after I heard the church bell five times.

"I bring you tray, but Mrs. McAuliff said no, you are to come down to supper."

"But I'm not hungry," I whined and rolled toward the wall.

"You come anyway," she said, and she tugged my arm to get me up.

She brought me into the dining room downstairs and I noticed a new, small table at the front. On it was white cake with blue flowers all over it. When I got closer, I could see it also had my name written on it!

Mrs. McAuliff stood up at her front table and said, "Girls, sing!"

They all sang happy birthday, which for some reason made me want to cry all over again, but I held it in. At 16, crying would definitely be a baby thing to do and I didn't feel like a baby today. I felt a hundred years old and, with all these girls, so very lonely.

After the singing, Mrs. McAuliff stepped over to give me a box and told me to open it.

"This present is from Mrs. Waite, the judge's wife, and Mrs. Wiborg on behalf of the Ladies Guild. They have all heard of your troubles."

Inside the box was a new pair of black boots. I could see they were new, not a smudge on them, and they had solid heels and the metal eyelets shone.

"Oh," was all I could manage to say.

"Now you are prepared for winter, finally. Those have to last now, until you leave us," Mrs. McAuliff said and she cut a piece of cake, put it on a small plate and handed it to me.

"We don't have cake for supper every day, do we, but this day is special. It feels like the New Year must bring you, and all of us, many better things."

CHAPTER 14

The month of January was so cold that none of the girls went outside much, except when we were assigned to check for eggs or milk cows. Right after my birthday I was assigned to the chickens.

Picking through their roosts, I would get to thinking and, after a few days of this I decided I was real mad at Aunt Hattie and at Pearl and Bernie for leaving me at Home School, even though I was learning how to get along with the mean girls and Mrs. MacAuliff. Mr. Hansen had said I would be on the baseball team in the spring if I was still here. But, I thought, I was certainly old enough to work at a real job and go help Aunt Hattie with Violet and the new baby. Or I could go work in the boarding house with Pearl and Bernie. Look at all the work I was doing here, after all.

The next Sunday when the Ladies Guild ladies came by, I saw Mrs. Waite again, who had helped me write the Christmas letters, and I thanked her for the birthday boots.

"Can we write another letter?" I asked her in the sitting room. "If you have paper I can write it myself."

"Certainly, dear. Let me find you some of my pretty stationary."

Ethelyn started the letter the way Miss Johnson had taught them in class.

Dear Aunt Hattie,
Thank you for the photo of Mama. I am sorry Mama died. If you brought Violet to your house, I can come to help take care of her

and the new baby. *What is the new baby's name? Is it a boy or a girl?*

Please write me here and tell me if I can come. I would need a train ticket please.

Your niece,
Ethelyn

Then on another sheet I wrote to Pearl:

Dear Pearl and Bernie,

I have been here almost four months now. I can sew, like you, and I know how to can pickles and do laundry. Please tell Aunt Sigrid I can come to work for her like you and Bernie. I won't be any trouble.

Mama died. Did Aunt Hattie write you? I think now we should take care of the new baby and Violet. All three of us can do it. Write me here and tell me when I can come.

Your sister,
Ethelyn

P.S. If you sent a coat, I did not get it, but I have one now. And boots.

Mrs. Waite took the letters and said she would mail them tomorrow. I pulled out my school notebook and began writing a list in the back of all the things I just knew I could do for Aunt Hattie and Pearl and Bernie, just so they would all know that I had become a grown-up while I'd been here at the school.

In February, Mrs. Wiborg took us Protestants to church like she did every Sunday and afterwards, when we were all sewing up holes in our stockings in the front

102

room, she stood up and clapped her hands to get our attention.

"Girls, I have some exciting news. The whole Ladies Guild will be with us next Sunday and we will all begin to make some very nice Easter dresses, since Easter is only six weeks away. They will bring us one pattern to share, but you will all have pretty new fabric to work with, now that the war is over. You will each sew your own special dress. And this will be a contest! The girl who sews the prettiest dress with the best stitching will win something very special."

"Oh, dear," Rosie whispered to me. "I can't sew pretty enough. I'll never win."

I told Rosie I thought she sewed better than most of the girls. "Even if we don't win, we will have new pretty dresses for Easter."

"I wonder what the prize will be," Rosie said. "Maybe an Easter bonnet? I saw a picture in a magazine of ladies in a parade all wearing these bonnets that went out to here."

She spread her arms wide over her head.

All of us spent the next Sunday with the Ladies Guild cutting out our patterns, and then we spent most evenings working on the dresses. Every Sunday, Mrs. Wiborg came by herself to help any of us who were having trouble. The pattern made a formal sailor-type dress with ruffles in the front, which Rosie said was all the rage in fashion now.

I realized the ribbon that had been attached to my Christmas box perfectly matched my Easter dress fabric, and then remembered the two dresses from home that I had long ago stuffed into my dresser drawer. I tried on the dresses one rest period when no one else was in the room and discovered I had outgrown them. I had gained weight since coming to the school and recovering from pneumonia.

The next evening, I found some ladies magazines that the Ladies Guild always left for us to read. I never looked at them, being too busy trying to finish my book, but I had a plan now. In an issue of Collier's, I found what I was looking for and spent the rest of the evenings that week off in a corner by myself, cutting paper patterns and arranging and re-arranging them on a small table.

The Sunday before Easter, we were supposed to wear our dresses in a kind of fashion show in the school's front room, for Mrs. Wiborg and the Ladies Guild. We stood at one end of the room and each lady examined each girl's dress closely, turning her this way and that. After inspection, the ladies moved to the dining room to compare notes and talk with the others. They closed the adjoining doors so we couldn't hear their comments. Rosie and I finally sat down together to await the announcement of the winner.

"Oh, Ethelyn, how did you ever do the hat? Nobody taught us hats," Rosie said, turning my head herself to see all around.

"Oh, I just copied from a magazine. It wasn't that hard. And I used one of my old dresses."

We all stood up when we saw Mrs. Wiborg lead the ladies back into the room. We expected the announcement of the winner and then the prize.

"Girls, we have made our decision, but we won't be announcing it here today. We're asking Pastor Walker at the church to help us with this during Easter services next Sunday. Won't that be nice?"

I was disappointed and so was Rosie. We would have to wait a whole week.

"Please just wear exactly what you have on now and be ready promptly at 9:45 next Sunday," Mrs. Wiborg said. "It will be a happy Easter, we promise."

CHAPTER 15

We filed into the church as usual on Easter morning, except our dresses made the old ladies turn their heads even further as we took our seats in the usual pews.

Mrs. Wiborg caught me as I was squeezing into the middle of one row and said, "Sit with me, dear, here at the end."

I wanted to sit with Rosie, but did as Mrs. Wiborg asked.

After the opening hymn, Pastor Walker stepped in front of the altar and said, "We have a special treat for you all today before our festive Easter service. Mrs. Wiborg?"

Mrs. Wiborg walked to the front and faced the congregation.

"My dear church, you may remember the fabric drive we had here during the Christmas season and now I'm pleased to show you its results." She paused. "You were all so generous."

"Girls, if you will all join me up here, quickly and quietly now."

I stood up and looked to my row to follow me. Rosie just shrugged her shoulders. As we assembled in an untidy line next to Mrs. Wiborg, she said, "Our Home School girls made fine work of the cloth from all your donations. Even while getting their usual school work and household chores done, they worked every Sunday and many, many evenings on the beautiful dresses you see them in today."

The congregation burst out in applause, which startled us all. Some of the girls tried to hide behind the girl next to them.

"They have learned valuable skills in doing this, skills that will serve them all well as they go away from us, which will be far too soon for my taste."

Some in the congregation chuckled at this.

"Our Ladies Guild met last week to judge the girls' dresses and feel so many of them are worthy of honors that it was difficult to choose. Therefore, they will now, each one of them, receive new spring shoes to wear to Sunday church as the days grow warm, and these will be provided to them back at the Home School this afternoon."

We all giggled as the congregation applauded again.

"But we did, ultimately, find one girl who we felt had done the finest work, and now I hand the young lady's name, and the announcement of her special prize, to Pastor Walker."

The pastor took a large envelop from Mrs. Wiborg and opened it, cleared his throat, and said, "Let us pray."

"Heavenly Father, we thank you for these girls among us and know that their improvement is entirely in your hands. We ask your blessing on them now and for each day of this coming Easter season."

He lifted his head and said, "He is risen!"

"He is risen, indeed!" the congregation answered him.

"And now, I am honored that Mrs. Wiborg has given me the task of bestowing our prize."

He pulled a small card from the envelope.

"Miss Ethelyn Gertrude Thompson."

I gasped. Rosie, who was standing next to me, jumped up and kissed my head, knocking my hat clear off.

"Ethelyn, can you come over to me please?" the pastor said.

While I struggled to put my hat back on, Mrs. Wiborg gave me a kiss on the cheek and moved me gently toward the pastor.

"Ethelyn, we are quite proud of your work and I see by this beautiful dress and matching bonnet why you deserve this honor," the pastor said.

He now pulled a certificate from the envelope.

"For her extraordinary seamstress and millinery skills, Ethelyn Thompson is awarded one semester of industrial sewing training at our esteemed Dunwoody Institute, to commence September 7, nineteen hundred and nineteen."

I was confused and looked over at Mrs. Wiborg's face at the far end of the line.

"It's all arranged, dear," Mrs. Wiborg said assuredly. The congregants chuckled again.

"Thank you, I..."

"You're quite welcome, Ethelyn. Much deserved."

I took the certificate from Pastor Walker and fumbled it as he tried to shake my hand.

"And now, our service of celebration."

Mrs. Wiborg took me by the hand and made me stop at the end of each pew that had a lady sitting at the end, so that each could admire my dress.

The other girls followed behind with the women murmuring appreciation as each passed and the organ struck the opening chords of the second hymn.

On the church steps after the service, Mrs. Wiborg clustered the girls all around the pastor for a group photo. "We'll send this to the papers, everyone!"

My hat blew off in the gust of warm spring air that whipped up just as the photographer snapped his camera.

The minute the group disbanded to return to Home School, I caught Mrs. Wiborg's elbow.

"But, will I have to leave Home School?" I asked her, thinking this Dunwoody place must be just like Home School only with more sewing lessons. Would I still be here in the fall and not with my family? These thoughts had distracted me throughout the service.

"Why no, dear, not until you are ready, and you're not quite ready. You'll be attending two schools in the fall, is all. Studies in the morning at Dunwoody, studies in the evenings, after chores, at the Home School."

I was so relieved and skipped right up to Rosie to tell her the good news.

"You're lucky. You'll still be sixteen," Rosie said. "They tell me I'll have to leave, come August. They're looking for a place to send me to work."

I hadn't thought of that. A fall without my friend at Home School.

CHAPTER 16

Shortly after Easter, Mrs. Hansen found me just as I was coming into the side kitchen from the chicken coop and she pulled a letter from her apron pocket. I read the postmark first. "Faribault" it said and a name I didn't know.

Dear Ethelyn,

I am sorry to tell you that your Aunt Hattie died in the sickness here, like so many others. Her husband died, too. Your sister, Violet, is fine and has been living with us since March 1. Your baby brother, Arnold, is with me also.

I have arranged that soon the two of them will move together to Chicago, where a nice lady has agreed to be their mother forever. Her name is Mabel Powers and, because you are old enough now, she says you may come to work for her and be with your little sister and brother.

Mrs. Powers needs time to get the little ones settled, but she says you could come to her next spring, after you turn 17. She will be writing to the headmistress of your school to make these arrangements very soon. Please write to me with your response.

Yours truly,
Mrs. Lars Engdahl
Faribault Care Home for Children

A job? My family in Chicago? I didn't know what to think. I certainly wanted to see Violet and meet Arnold. Would Mrs. Powers be nice to work for? She wouldn't be my mother, would she? I am too old to need a mother. Pearl and Bernie had, it seemed, forgotten about me entirely. This was certainly a kind offer from a stranger.

Mrs. McAuliff had explained I would start my formal training at the Dunwoody Institute in the fall, but would still be part of the Home School family until my next birthday in January. By now, though, a lot of the girls who had been living here when I first arrived were gone. Bergit. Dorethea. Karen. Sarah, the team pitcher, was still here and Rosie. In August, Rosie would leave us, too. They had found a position for her as a domestic with a wealthy, Catholic family in St. Cloud.

"Domestic," Rosie had sneered when she got the letter a few weeks ago. "Cooking, cleaning, wiping dirty noses. Ish."

I realized that is what I would face if I accepted Mrs. Powers' offer to go to Chicago to be with Violet and Arnold. Still, they were my family. It would be different than Rosie's situation. But I did wonder if there was any point in going through with sewing training at the Institute. Would it be a waste of time? When would I ever sew again if I went off to Chicago? For the first time in my life somebody was offering me choices. I didn't really think I was able to make one.

CHAPTER 17

In early May on a Saturday after preparing the garden for planting, Mr. Hansen told us girls it was time to become a baseball team and took us out to the field on the side where the cows weren't grazing. Still the grass was already high and it was hard to walk through, let alone run to catch a ball.

A new girl, a Negro named Winny, had arrived at the school and Rosie and I quickly heard from her that she was a good batter. We told Mr. Hansen this because Winny was too shy to say anything, and today we brought her out to Mr. Hansen's field.

Mr. Hansen first set a brick down in the grass. Then he moved three girls out to where he said first, second and third base were. Rosie was at second base. He set two more girls behind them farther out, one between first and second base, and one between second and third base. He gave the ball to Sarah and placed her on a pretend pitcher's mound, because everyone already knew she would be the pitcher. He returned to his home base brick.

"New girl," Mr. Hansen said. "Winny? You our batter now."

The girl just shook her head, but Rosie stepped up to her. "Come on, Winny. None of us can bat good."

Winny took the bat from Mr. Hansen without a word and stood at the brick.

"Okay Ethelyn, you our catcher!"

He put an apron type of thing over my head and it was heavy on my chest, like the x-ray machine from the infirmary had been. It made me lean forward on my toes when I bent down like Mr. Hanson showed me.

"And hold those hands out in front like so."

I did as he showed me.

"Now, you only watch Sarah. Watch her hands, just like you do for catching all the time."

"I'm going to run bases for Winny. Ready? Pitch," he hollered and Sarah got ready to throw the ball. "Over the brick, now."

Sarah threw and the ball came almost over the brick, to my right. I had to lean over to grab it from the dirt. Winny hadn't moved a muscle.

"Ball one," Mr. Hansen called.

I threw the ball back to Sarah and she pitched it again. Winnie swung and the ball went fast on the ground over near second base. The first and second base girls looked at each other, deciding which one should go get it and neither of them did.

"Girls! Girls!" Mr. Hansen was running to first base now. Finally, Judy picked up the ball and ran over to second base just in time to tag Mr. Hansen's leg. He was "out." It looked to me like maybe he ran slower than he could.

"Good now. Winny bat again and I'll run again."

We played for a long time, all the while with me as the catcher. By the end of the day, the girls at first, second and third base got a little better at getting the balls that Winny kept hitting and hitting.

Two more Saturdays the girls were allowed to play after the gardening chores and laundry were done. On the last Saturday in May, Mr. Hansen said we were going to walk to the ball field that was a little ways down the block toward the streetcar line. When we got there, we were surprised to find another group of girls standing around and throwing balls back and forth.

Mr. Hansen went up to talk to a lady who was with the girls. The lady was wearing white bloomers, which I had only ever seen ladies in the magazines do.

Pretty soon the lady and Mr. Hansen told us that we would play a real game today, only three innings. "Usually it will be six, but you all have chores to do so we can't play long," Mr. Hanson said.

There were seven Home School girls and they had seven girls, but the others all wore matching outfits, white bloomers like the lady and a long red sash that went around their necks and came down their fronts like a tie. They were like pretty sailor suits, which so many girls from regular families wore. They all had real baseball gloves that fit their hands perfectly. On the Home School side, I was the only one with a glove, the special catcher's mitt from Mr. Hanson.

With Sarah pitching and me catching, Rosie played second base.

Mr. Hansen said his girls would bat first, which I thought was a terrible idea. We had hardly practiced batting, except for Winny who was already so good at it.

Rosie batted first and the pitcher the others girls had was very fast. Rosie got three strikes in a row. Then it was my turn and my hands were so sweaty they stuck to the wooden bat. I let the first ball go by, but then hit the next one. It went over to the right where Mr. Hansen was standing, a foul ball. Two more times I swung and missed completely.

The next girl to bat got out too, so it was time to switch sides. As we passed the other girls coming in from the field, one girl with gold ribbons in her hair stuck her tongue out at Rosie. "Ha, ha," she said. Rosie gave her the raspberries right back.

I took my place at home plate, which was a real baseball home plate like I had seen in photographs.

Sarah tried to pitch harder than usual and this just made the ball go crazy. I had to get up and run to get it many times before the first girl hit it once. The ball went over by third base, but the Home School girl missed it and it rolled a long way behind her. The batter girl got to second base because of that. The next girl to bat hit the first pitch Sarah threw and it went way over everybody's head, way out behind second base where nobody was standing. It was a home run and the bloomer girls now had two runs.

By the end of the first inning, my knees ached badly from all the up and down I had done. The inning lasted a long time. The other girls had eight runs by the end of it.

At the bottom of the second inning, Winny was finally up to bat. The Home School girls already had two outs. Winny hit a home run, but she was the only one who got to cross home base.

It was a humiliating loss for us, even if it was only three innings. Afterwards, the lady in the bloomers made her girls shake hands with each of us and while we were doing that she went to a picnic basket in the grass and brought out a pitcher and glasses and poured lemonade for everyone. Up to then I was ready to not play baseball again, but I loved lemonade.

Walking back to the house, Mr. Hansen told us we would only practice batting next Saturday.

"Just batting. We practice lots," he said.

115

CHAPTER 18

The remainder of May, when we weren't tilling the garden, we all practiced our batting with Mr. Hansen, even in the cool evenings as the daylight lingered. During the school's end-of-school picnic on June 1, Mr. Hansen clapped his hands for our attention.

"Girls, I have big news," he said. "We will be a real team now! We join the city league and play other girls, all summer!"

When we stopped clapping, he said that the league included the Pillsbury girls, who had beat us so badly three weeks ago, but also teams from the YWCA, the Mission Home, Ebenezer House and neighborhood groups from Polish Town, Camden and Bohemian Flats. We would have a full schedule starting next week and leading to a championship game in August.

That evening, Rosie and I sat sewing in the living room and discussed this exciting news. A full summer of baseball!

"But we don't got no uniforms, like them fancy girls had," Rosie lamented. "The red sashes and bloomers! Oh, their outfits were adorable, even though I hate those girls."

"Well, why can't we have uniforms?" I said. "We can all sew?"

"We don't have no fabric for that," Rosie argued. "After our Easter dresses, the church isn't going to give us more."

"I'll ask Mrs. Wiborg. She'll help us, I know she will," I said.

On Sunday, I waited for a moment while Mrs. Wiborg chatted with the pastor, then I caught up to walk beside her at the back of the group walking home.

"We just really must have uniforms to be a proper team," I told her. "Rosie and I, and some of the other girls I bet, could sew them. They look real easy to me."

"Ethelyn, I can't promise anything, but you have a good idea," Mrs. Wiborg said. "Let me ask around and see if I can get someone to donate the fabric."

I skipped forward to tell Rosie right then and there, and Rosie skipped back and gave Mrs. Wiborg a hug around her big hips.

Mrs. Wiborg did better than get fabric donated. She got Mr. Hansen a patron for his team. She came wandering out to the mucky practice field in her Sunday shoes one rainy day to tell us as we hit ball after ball that Sarah pitched to us.

"Girls, the Kickernick Company in downtown Minneapolis has agreed to give us the material and lend us their name to become a true team for the league games coming up."

"Hooray!" we all shouted.

Mr. Hansen asked, "What is this patron, Mrs. Wiborg?"

"That means your expenses will be paid. Gloves, bats, anything you need, and all that they ask in return is for us to use their name and sew it onto the uniform sashes, to tell the world of their generosity."

"Yes...?" Mr. Hansen didn't seem to understand. "We no pay?"

Mrs. Wiborg turned to us and clapped her hands. "From now on you girls will be known as The Kickernicks!"

Rosie and I hugged and couldn't stop jumping up and down. We agreed that Kickernicks sounded like a good team of ball players.

"Somebody who will knock you right out of your knickers, right?" Rosie said.

"We start sewing like mad tonight, girls," Mrs. Wiborg said. "So don't wear yourselves out today."

Rosie was right. All the girls were so good at hand-stitching by now that the bloomers and tops were easy work once we had the pattern down. And the fabric we got, though again a kind of navy blue that I didn't really like, was light enough that our needles went through it like butter, without fraying. We had four outfits made within a week, with one more week to go before we had to debut them in a game against Ebenezer. The last part, however, would be the sashes. We would have to trace and cut out the letters using a different, stiffer fabric, and then sew each and every letter on by hand, using our best, smallest stitches, seven times. The nine letters of K-I-C-K-E-R-N-I-C-K.

"It's going to take years!" Rosie moaned when the team had spent most of the next evening working on them and only succeeded in cutting out half of the necessary letters. Mrs. Wiborg had assigned Rosie, Judy and me, as the best hand-stitchers, to the task of attaching them, while the other girls continued with the uniforms and letter cutting.

We were now allowed to practice for two hours in the middle of the day, counting as our lunch break and rest periods, and otherwise had to tend to our summer chores in the garden and barns. There was no time to rest. Mrs. Hansen kept a close eye on us, but she also made sure to give the girls who were not on the team the longer, more difficult Home School chores. At night, everyone sewed and sewed and tried to ignore Mrs. Hansen's lights out bell.

Wearing the uniforms really did seem to make us into a better team, I thought. While we were always good catchers, we were now batting well, too, and not just Winny. Mr. Hansen said it was a miracle, but Rosie said it was because we had sewn magic into the letters of "Kickernick."

Throughout the summer league season, games were held twice a week. The plan was that by the end of summer, every team played every other team at least twice.

By mid-August, the Kickernicks were ranked Number 3 in the city league and if we won just two more games, we would go up against the Number 1 team, the Pillsburys, the ones we had played and lost to way back in May.

With just three games to go until the end of summer, it happened to be Rosie who hit the winning run. She turned out to be a lousy infielder, but a great batter, hitting a home run when three girls, including Winny, were on base.

With the Kickernicks now Number 2 in the league, Mr. Kickernick himself showed up to the next game we were to play against the Camden girls. Mrs. Wiborg brought him over to the team bench just before the game was to start.

Mr. Kickernick stood in front of us, looking pretty silly and hot in his business suit.

"You make me proud, like a father, in your beautiful uniforms bearing my company's name. Go out there and win this for all the poor girls in this city who will never get this chance, and do it for me. Can you do that?"

We all hollered out, "Yes!" though I'm not sure we felt sure of it at the moment. We were all too nervous.

He chuckled a little bit and then stuck his cigar back in his mouth and moved over to the stands behind home plate to watch the game.

I got lucky in the sixth inning, with the score at 3 to 2, in favor of Camden. They had one girl on base when their batter hit directly at Rosie at second. Rosie fumbled the ball at first, giving the girl time to head toward third, but Rosie got the ball to me at home in time to tag the girl out. At the bottom of the inning, Winny got to second and Rosie hit a home run to win the game. The Home School girls were going to the championship game.

Mr. Kickernick came over to shake Mr. Hansen's hand, while Mrs. Wiborg lined us all up to be congratulated by him, as well.

When it was my turn to shake Mr. Kickernick's hand, Mrs. Wiborg told him, "Our home run hitter, Rosie, and Ethelyn, our catcher here, sewed on every one of your letters by hand. Aren't they beautiful?"

"You are to be commended," the man said. "It's fine work. Fine, Ethelyn."

He lifted the sash draped over my chest, fingering the letters a long time. "Yes, fine work. I will see you at the next game--wouldn't miss it--and the Kickernicks are going to win, right?"

"Right, sir," I said as he moved on to another girl.

On the day of the final game, Mr. Hansen stood in front of us, our uniforms clean and pressed fresh by Mrs. Hansen, a big job that had taken all the day before to complete.

"You have done a good thing," Mr. Hansen said. "Zehr gut. If we don't win today, I still love you all. You are like my own daughters, if I only had a daughter."

We all hugged him until he said, "Genuf. Play ball!"

The Pillsbury team took the field, the sparkling white of their uniforms nearly blinding us in the August sun. There wasn't a cloud in the sky, yet the humidity was so high that we were all soaked through before we began, dark navy not being the best color for heat.

While we tossed balls and swung bats to warm up, I noticed the Pillsbury coach lady, who had served us lemonade back in May, bringing a young man over to meet Mr. Hansen. I thought he must be another coach. He smiled broadly at Mr. Hansen, who was nodding and pointing the stranger toward third base. The young man turned to holler and wave to the Home School girls.

"Good luck now, girls. Let the best team win!" he yelled. He took his position to the side of third base and it was time to play.

The game was tied at the end of the fifth inning and, since they only played six innings, we Kickernicks got very jittery. Sarah paced up and down her pitcher's mound. Rosie took her long red pigtails into her mouth at second, and Mr. Hansen rubbed his head over and over at his position watching first base.

The Pillsburys were batting at the top of the sixth and Sarah managed to strike out the first two of their girls. The third one, however, hit a fly ball so far out past center field that nobody could have jumped high enough to catch it. With that one run, the Kickernicks had to get at least two runs when it was our turn at the bottom of the inning.

"Please let it stay at two," I prayed silently from my post behind the plate. "Two, two, two."

The fourth batter for the Pillsburys was a chunky girl with gold ribbons in her hair. Sarah struck her out in three pitches and the Kickernicks were off the bench to switch sides. Rosie would be the third batter for the bottom of the sixth; I would be first, with Winny in between.

As I turned from my catcher's post to choose a bat, I noticed Mr. Kickernick standing behind the fence at home plate.

"Good girl, Ethelyn. Win it now," he hollered to me and I think I saw him wink.

I was up to the plate, feeling Mr. Kickernick's eyes on my back the whole time. I struck out.

"Ah, bum luck," the boy coach from the Pillsbury team called over to me from his position watching third base. He smiled and waved a little when I noticed him.

"That's okay, Ethy," Rosie said at the bench. "We'll still get 'em."

Winny was next up and she hit the first pitch thrown to her. It sped past the third base girl at ground level and ended up in deep left field where no one seemed to be. Winny had learned to hit a ball anywhere she wanted it to go. She was stopped, safely, at second base and now Rosie was up.

Rosie wasted no time. On the first pitch, she hit a fly ball 50 feet over the right fielder's head and Winny was home in a split second. Rosie, not too far behind her, hit home plate. Two runs! No need to play anymore.

We all rushed to home plate and jumbled up with hugs and jumping. Mr. Hansen joined us and we tried to lift him up all together, but he just laughed and shouted, "Nein, nein, nein!"

Mrs. Wiborg and even Mrs. McAuliff came over from their seats in the stands and shook hands with each girl. "You have made the Home School proud, girls," Mrs. McAuliff said.

Mrs. Wiborg turned away just as Mr. Kickernick, their sponsor, came up to me.

"You're not just an excellent seamstress, but a good ball player," he said. "Mrs. Wiborg tells me you'll be trained at Dunwoody. What will you do after that?"

"I may go to Chicago to be with my brother and sister," I answered without thinking.

"You might consider coming to work for me," he said. "I always need girls."

"Well, I..."

"Give it a think, little lady," he said, and moved over to the lemonade table, where Mrs. Hansen had arrived with a celebration cake, too.

CHAPTER 19

Rosie was leaving Home School in a week. After the championship game, I spent as much time as I could with her, but I also slipped up to my room with a match for the lantern as early as I could. I was working on a hat for Rosie and Mrs. Hansen had given me special permission to stay up late to finish it.

"Look at me," Rosie said on the day she was to leave. "I got real ladies gloves and everything."

The Catholic family had included the gloves, along with Rosie's train ticket to St. Cloud, in a package earlier in the week. I had seen them and knew I could design a hat to match exactly.

"Take this. It's my thank you, finally, for getting my watch back." I handed Rosie the package as she picked up her suitcase. "You'll write to me. Promise now," I said, telling myself I wasn't going to cry. I clung on to one of her gloved hands.

"Ah, you know I don't like writing," Rosie said. "When you become a working lady, too, you can take the train up to see me."

"Sure I will."

She put on the hat, looked in the hall mirror and said, "Now don't I look right out of Collier's Magazine."

We hugged a long time because I was not able to speak any more.

Mrs. McAuliffe finally had to pull Rosie away. "The train will be coming," she said.

On the first Monday in September, I was to begin my training at the Dunwoody Institute, five mornings a week. I would get there by myself on the streetcar and return to Home School in time for afternoon chores and getting school assignments from Miss Johnson and Mrs. Arnold, the math teacher. I would do the schoolwork in the evenings in the dining room, while the other girls played or sewed in the living room. I would take my lunch with me in a pail and eat it after class, before taking the streetcar back from Dunwoody.

I recited these plans to myself at night in my bed to be sure I wouldn't forget anything. Then I realized the last time I had ridden a streetcar by myself had been the day I tried to jump onto the train.

When the day came, I was out the door at seven in the morning, checking and rechecking my instructions, the streetcar schedule and my dress. The minute I stepped off the streetcar at Dunwoody I was astonished at how big a place it was. Its stone steps up to the main entrance seemed higher than any I'd ever walked. My worry got only a little better by finding the the registration office just inside the door.

I stood in a long line of girls at the registration window, trying to look like I knew exactly what I was doing. Finally, the woman behind the window took the papers from me, stamped them, and pointed to a row of chairs just down the long hallway. "Someone will be by soon to lead you to sewing," the woman said. "Don't go wandering off."

I sat and fidgeted, flipping the handle on my lunch pail. It gave a little bang each time and I jumped each time. I scanned down the long hallway in one direction and didn't notice the boy in striped overalls who had come up to me from the other direction.

"You can't eat that yet. I don't care how hungry you are," the boy said, a silly grin on his face.

"No, I..." I began.

"I'm just teasing, doll. I know we got a new term starting. Your first day?"

"Yes. It is," I managed to say. Then I think I saw this boy's protruding ears wiggle back and forth.

"You don't remember me, do you?" the boy said.

I was distracted by his ears, and then thought how few boys I ever had seen lately. "Um, no. Do I know you?"

"Baseball...the Pillsbury's game a few weeks ago? I was coaching third base and lugging the equipment for them. I even congratulated you and you said 'thanks'."

"Oh, I'm sorry..."

"I never forget a pretty face, especially one behind a catcher's mask."

The boy turned then to greet three more girls who were coming over to sit.

"I'm to take you all to sewing," he announced with a little bow. "Ladies, my name is Einar and this is a really big place. We don't want anybody getting lost, especially this doll here, who is really hungry," he gestured toward me.

"I am not..."

"Get up, hon. Everybody follow me," and Einar spun down the hallway with us girls struggling to keep up behind him.

I grabbed my pail and pocketbook while also trying to smooth my dress as I stood. I had so wanted to wear my Easter dress to show off the sewing that had gotten me to this place, but the weather had turned very chill overnight. Mrs. Hanson had insisted I put on my one last dress from home. I had worked on it over the summer to let it out, but it was still a little tight. The dress was embarrassing especially considering the beautiful green silk one worn by one of the other new sewing girls in our little group.

Einar was ten steps ahead of everybody already, talking back at us over his shoulder.

As we passed a hard steel door on the left, he paused and said, "That's where I spend my day, so when you want to come have some manly company, stop in here to the sheet metal gang. They'll be good to you, I promise."

He turned around then and began walking backwards.

"Me, now, I can't be trusted," and he did, in fact, wiggle his ears back and forth. I had not imagined it. Two of the other girls giggled at this.

Einar stopped dead in his backwards tracks and leaned forward to grab my free hand. "Come on, we'll be late," and he spun, pulling me behind him.

Einar turned one corner and then, after another long hallway, turned another. I just knew I'd never find my way back and wondered if this boy would come to escort us at the end of class. Finally he stopped us at two huge wooden doors. Einar let go of my hand and turned to the group, leaning a little on the right hand door, and said, "This is my stop. You ladies, enjoy your day."

He grabbed my hand again and gave it a quick kiss before letting go.

"I'll see you later," and he pushed the big door open, holding it, and motioned for us all to go through.

I gasped when we got inside and I saw how big the room was. There must have been 50 shiny black sewing machines on 50 black metal tables that seemed to stretch the length of a baseball field toward the back. A single light bulb hung over each machine from a long wire in the tall ceiling. Still the room was dim and shadowy. Half the tables, toward the back, were already occupied by girls who did not look up from their work when we entered. Their machines whirred.

I wondered how on earth I would learn to operate a sewing machine. All my sewing had been fine, hand-stitching. There were no sewing machines at Home School. A woman with hair piled high on her head entered from a side door.

"Ladies, please choose your machine in the front row. You'll see your name on a little card on the chairs," she said. "Try not to bother the others in back who are working now. Don't be a nuisance."

I looked at the black-haired girl next to me, the one in the green silk dress. She shrugged her shoulders, but started toward the front row, motioning for me to follow her.

"Here's mine," the girl whispered to me as we reached the first machine. "Where are you?"

I saw my name was on the very next chair and moved behind the girl.

"Oh, great. We'll be pals then. Neighbors," the girl whispered. "I'm Zena, by the way."

"Girls, please!" the teacher said loudly and shooed the rest of the girls toward the machines.

Zena and I sat side by side and, as the lady turned toward a blackboard at the front, I leaned over to say, "I'm Ethelyn and I'm scared to death."

Zena made a face at me and mouthed, "Me, too," and giggled.

The woman in charge stood stock still at the front, waiting for all of us to turn our attention to her.

"Girls, by Friday, you will operate these machines as well as the girls behind you. We have the most modern equipment here and it is all designed to make our work easy."

"You'll find if you just pay attention, you'll be working girls in no time." The woman shouted and craned her neck to the back of the room. "Isn't that right, girls?"

"Yes, Mrs. Kickernick," some of them said as they barely looked up from their machines, not interested.

Kickernick? Our team? This woman must be the wife of the man sponsoring our baseball team, I thought.

"New girls, now listen. The girls behind you are getting paid for their work, but they don't get paid if they spend their days chatting with all of you." She shouted again. "Workers? Go back to what you were doing, please."

"Now, I am Mrs. Kickernick and we will be together, as you know, until December. I expect you here every day with no excuses. Understand?"

I guessed we were supposed to answer her, as I had learned with our Home School teachers.

"Yes, Mrs. Kickernick," I said, and my cheeks got hot when I realized none of the other girls had responded. The teacher looked over her glasses at me as she continued talking.

"If you are in this class that means someone has decided your hand-stitching shows promise. We'll see about that. Machine work can be even finer than anything you have done, so we don't expect any pride here. We expect hard work and beautiful sewing that our manufacturers can be proud to sell to the people of this city and beyond."

I caught Zena's eye again and she touched the shoulder of her emerald green dress and whispered, "I made this all by hand and I'm damned proud of it."

"On your right you'll find a little drawer where we keep spools of thread. You only have white for now." Mrs. Kickernick continued. "On your left, a drawer with squares of fabric. Again, you only have white muslin to work with until you prove yourselves."

Mrs. Kickernick then pulled a large chart down over the blackboard and began, with a long wooden pointer, to name every part on a diagram of a Singer sewing machine, the same machine that sat in front of each girl. I so wanted to have pencil and paper to write down the names of the parts. How was I going to remember them otherwise? I raised my hand and Mrs. Kickernick stopped in her pointing and, looking annoyed, said, "Yes? Your name is…"

"Ethelyn, ma'am," I said. "May we have something to write this down?"

"No. You will remember this soon enough," Mrs. Kickernick said and turned back to the diagram.

When she was through with the parts of the machine, she turned and said, "After my demonstration of threading, you will all sit quietly while I go to each of you, one by one, to get you started. The rest of you will wait your turn in silence. Study the chart and then study your machine."

When the teacher was done at her own machine in the front, she moved to the front row of new girls and began at the far end away from me and Zena, giving us a chance to whisper to each other again.

"Wasn't that boy darling, the one who led us here?" Zena said.

"I don't know," I said. "He was kind of gangly looking, wasn't he?" I did think he was funny, though, and I touched my hand where he had kissed it. He was the first boy to give me a kiss of any kind, except of course. Papa, who had kissed the top of my head every morning.

"I didn't know there would be boys here," I admitted to Zena, keeping an eye out for Mrs. Kickernick's approach. "There are only girls at my other school."

"You go to another school? I'm just here because my mama made me come. I plan to get married as soon as I can. How come you're at school?"

"I live there and my family is all gone. I mean, living elsewhere."

Zena said, "My papa drinks and ends up in jail. That's why mama says I have to work and bring home some money soon. She plans to divorce him the minute I'm making money. That's what she says. Isn't it a scandal?" But Zena giggled a little when she said this.

Mrs. Kickernick clapped her hands down at the end of the row. "Ssh. Didn't I say 'Silence'?"

131

She was glaring at us. "You will sit silently until I come to you."

I turned from Zena and tested the wheel on the left side of the machine. It made the needle go up and down. Then I pressed on the pedal I noticed at my feet and the machine gave a whir, its needle suddenly bobbing up and down. I gasped.

"New girls, please don't touch the machine until I come by!"

Embarrassed again, I put my hands in my lap and stared at the big clock on the wall. It was only 9 a.m. I would be here three more hours in what already felt like a full day of school.

Mrs. Kickernick carried a little chair with her from girl to girl and when she got to my place, she sat it down next to me and told me to move onto it. She then sat in my chair and showed me how to thread the needle, how the motor began working the minute the pedal was pressed, how it slowed or sped up depending on the amount of pressure on that floor pedal and another at her right knee. She showed how the wheel on the left was used to move the needle without the pedals. Finally, she touched the metal guard that held the fabric down while also protecting one's fingers from the needle.

"A puncture is points off your grade," Mrs. Kickernick said. "A smart seamstress never has accidents."

She had carried a square of black cloth with her and now put it under the needle and ran the fabric through the machine so fast I couldn't see the needle working. When she was finished, she showed me the straight, tiny white stitches from one end to the other.

"Study this," she barked and stood up, moving her stool over to Zena. She turned back to me and said, "Now you will practice on that one fabric until noon. You're the one from Home School, is that right?"

"Yes, ma'am" I said.

"We'll see if you've learned anything there. You're the first to come to us from Home School. So many trouble-making girls in this city. It's a shame, is what it is."

I opened my mouth to say I wasn't a trouble-maker, but Mrs. Kickernick was already moving Zena to the little chair and threading the needle on Zena's machine.

At noon, a whistle sounded and the working girls at the rear of the room all pushed their chairs back at once, the chairs making a scraping, screeching sound on the wooden floor. They all reached under their machines to grab lunch pails that looked just like mine. My neck and shoulders ached from bending over the machine for two hours straight, watching the needle too much, I realized, not watching my stitches or the fabric. I threaded and rethreaded and started over and over. The small fabric square was now covered with raggedly lines of stitching, loose ends sticking up here and there. I so wanted to pull them all out and put them back in with a needle, properly by hand.

"Leave your cloth pinned with your name card in the basket as you leave, new girls," Mrs. Kickernick said. "Those who need to wait for your ride may eat down the hall in the canteen."

I had a half hour before the streetcar would pass by. I followed Zena out the door.

"Zena, will you eat?" I asked her out in the hallway.

"I have nothing," the girl said.

"I have enough to share," I offered. "We've just finished pickles and cucumbers at my school, and I have bread and jam."

Zena followed me without another word.

In the canteen, we sat at a table by ourselves and I pulled out the food, all folded in a cloth napkin, the pickles and cucumber wrapped again in paper.

"Help yourself," I said, pushing the napkin toward Zena.

"Where do you get so much food?" Zena's eyes were wide.

"The Home School," she said. "That's where I live."

"Were you bad?"

"My papa died. My sisters moved away, and Mama, and then she died. It was the sickness, you know."

I pushed the paper full of pickles toward Zena, but she reached for the bread and tore off half. She stuffed it into her mouth and said, "This is good. Wish I had coffee."

Einar, the boy with the wiggly ears, was suddenly behind Zena, looking over her head at me.

"Coffee? Why allow me," he said. He produced a thermos bottle.

"Shall I pour?"

CHAPTER 20

My streetcar got me to Dunwoody each morning 15 minutes before class started, so I found my way to the canteen where, I soon learned, Einar usually ate his breakfast, a large spread of cheese and meat that came from his father's small grocery on Cedar Avenue. My second day there he had explained to me, while sharing some of his food, that he would become a union sheet metal worker at the turn of the year. He was in his last stretch of classes this fall and was the most senior student in his group, though the youngest. This, he liked to say, gave him added privileges and duties, like escorting the groups of girl students. His program took two years to complete and he had been allowed early entrance because of the war.

"With all the boys off fighting, there was a time I was the only one in the program," he told me that day.

He was too young to fight, but had a brother killed overseas.

When I expressed my sympathies, he said, "At least my mother didn't live long enough even to see him go. And, we were lucky. We lost no one to the Spanish flu at least."

So of course I had to tell him about Papa and how we all got scattered everywhere after he died.

Last Friday, the end of my first week, Einar told me how Dunwoody staged a Harvest ball, the first Saturday in October. It was a way for all the students at the huge school to meet each other.

"Won't you be my date?" he said at breakfast.

He was so funny looking, and funny. "I'm not sure if the Home School allows it," I managed to say, though I knew I did want to go.

"Why not check with the lady in charge?" he said. "Tell her I'm good for it."

I asked Mrs. McAulliff about it that very afternoon and she said she would give me her answer only after meeting Einar's father and talking it over. She knew of the grocery over on Cedar Avenue and would go over there one day this week.

When our weekend's usual chores of laundry, gardening and church were done, I began to worry just what I would wear to a Harvest Ball dance and looked through my growing bundle of fabric scraps, ribbons and what remained of my old dresses. The only possibility among them was my winning Easter dress, though it was hopelessly out of season, of course. Perhaps I could find a way to give it a matching coat, one of the long, lined ones I saw many fancy women wearing downtown these days.

On Wednesday afternoon, as I came in from class, Mrs. McAuliff found me in the kitchen to report on her conversation with Mr. Bertelsen, Einar's father, who had spoken to her in English and Danish, she said.

"We got along fine, Ethelyn, and he gives his permission for you to be escorted by his boy," she said. "I have also talked to the dance chairwoman at Dunwoody, who assures me the event will be well chaperoned. You can take the streetcar there, but I'll pick you up in my motor car when it's done."

"Thank you, Mrs. McAuliff." My thoughts immediately swirled between making a proper dress and learning how to dance.

Classes at Dunwoody had already become a sort of boring routine. Mrs. Kickernick started each one by showing us another special stitch the machines could do, special ways we could hold the fabric under the powerful needle to get a new effect. Then she left us to work on our own. We graduated quickly to the fancier fabrics, though still they were remnants and cast-offs, and we completed the day's assignment by pinning our names to the new creations and dropping them in a large basket by the door as we were dismissed.

I happened to notice one day that Mrs. Kickernick's own desk had a basket where she deposited our projects after they were graded, which gave me an idea. I told Zena to go ahead and meet me in the canteen a little later, after I approached Mrs. Kickernick, who was making checkmarks in the worn leather ledger she always kept open on her desk.

"What becomes of our old assignments here, Mrs. Kickernick?" I asked, gesturing to the basket next to her.

"What?" she looked up over her spectacles at me. "Oh, it's you, is it? I take those off to the girls in the back who make use of them one way or another. Why?"

"It's just I want to make a coat for an outfit I'm working on at home. I have no money, but I could make something for you, if you like, or do some extra credit work? If I could have a look and maybe find something that will work for the coat?"

"My husband told me about you," she said, which baffled me. "The baseball player, right?"

"Yes, ma'am," I said. "That seems a long time ago. He was so generous to give our team so much material and equipment."

"Generous. Yes, well," she went back to studying her ledger. "Go ahead and have a look. It's against my policies, but I know you Home School girls are too poor to manage much. Go on ahead."

She waved her fountain pen at the basket of fabrics.

With an armful of some fabrics I just knew would make a good coat lining, and some other promising finds, I saw my evenings up until the dance were going to be fully occupied with my creation.

The dance. Practicing waltzes with Rosie in the Home School's sitting room had probably not prepared me for the Harvest Ball. With no boys around, how could us girls really know we were getting it right, and none of us could ever remember who was to be the boy and who the girl. And any of the modern steps? We surely didn't have those records for our Vitrola. Rosie was gone now. I had no one to practice with me. I hoped Einar would be content sipping punch on the sidelines, or would he have to find other girls to dance with?

I had to make do with an added ruffle around the neck of my Easter dress to make it more appropriate for fall. The coat came together nicely with the help of a donation from Sarah, our team pitcher, who was happy to give me a heavy winter dress she had from her home. "I wish I never had to wear another dress in my life," she told me. "Bloomers are the thing, I think."

It was a scramble to get it all done, but two days before the dance I was able to bring my creation in to

Dunwoody to show Zena. She said the coat and dress looked right out of the pages of Collier's.

"You're so lucky to get to go. Who am I going to meet sitting in this dingy sewing room half the day, the other half holding my mother's hand?" she said.

Mrs. Wiborg made a rare appearance upstairs at the Home School on Saturday and found me getting ready in my room. She waved a curling iron in one hand and a scissors in the other.

"Sit, dear. I will do your hair. I used to do my own daughters."

"That's awfully kind of you. I don't know how to do anything with it except my pigtails."

"We'll manage," Mrs. Wiborg said. "Pigtails certainly will not do on this occasion."

Many pins, snips, curls and tucks later, I didn't recognize myself in the mirror and worried that Einar wouldn't either, or wouldn't like what he saw. I looked like a city lady! I wished I didn't have to cover my new bob with the hat, but knew it would be improper to attend a dance without one.

Earlier in the week Mrs. McAuliff decided, after I modeled the dress and coat for her, that she would drive me to the dance as well, she saying that my dress would get mussed on the streetcar.

"I know exactly what time the dance ends and will pick you up myself," the matron continued. "We won't have you riding the streetcars at that time of night on a Saturday, God knows."

"Besides, you're going to look so beautiful, we don't want some other boy whisking you off the streetcar and away from this Einar fellow," she said.

I don't think I'd ever seen Mrs. McAuliff's eyes brighten so much as they did when she said that. It was funny to think of that day I first met her, me covered in railroad soot, with my busted boots and being as rude to her as I possibly could be.

Out on the street, Mrs. McAuliff opened her car door for me and I just stood there looking inside.

"It's fine, dear. I've been driving since these machines were invented, goodness knows," she said. I didn't tell her I had never been in a motor car.

I examined the dials and gear shift as she drove through Minneapolis, thinking it all looked far more complicated than my Dunwoody sewing machine.

"Be out here promptly at 10:45," she said as I stepped out of the car.

Einar spotted me the second I came in the door to the gymnasium. He had been waiting just inside holding a corsage big enough to cover my chest.

"My, it's like my catcher's apron!" I teased him.

"Much more becoming on you, I hope," and he gave it to me to pin on. "I'm no good at that stuff."

"Wherever did you get such a big one?" I asked.

"My father runs a store, remember? I traded the florist across the street for a crate of tomatoes. Old Pops is none the wiser."

"How romantic," I said, and managed to get the giant flowers pinned on, the work of my new ruffle nearly hidden now.

Turns out Einar was an excellent dancer who had benefited from the teachings of a girl cousin. He was patient enough to teach me a thing or two and we danced every dance. When other fellows asked to cut in, he just spun me away saying, "Stick with me, doll. I know all the moves."

CHAPTER 21

The sewing girls who had begun their schooling in September were to move to the back rows, where the working girls were, on November 1, as a sign that they had progressed enough in their skills to get paid a small stipend for producing actual undergarments. Other new students would take their places at the front.

Mrs. Kickernick explained that the working section of the classroom was a testing ground, to see if they could keep up a steady pace now that they knew the fundamentals, and would their garments be good enough for selling to the public. A quota was set for them to meet each day, increasing each two or three days, with Mrs. Kickernick tallying and examining what lay in the basket at each girl's feet at the end of the day. Those who did the best would be offered a position at the Kickernick Company, run by her husband.

"Only four positions will be open there after your graduation. If you don't do well, you'll have to go hunting for a position on your own," she warned.

As Mrs. Kickernick had predicted, Zena and I had mastered our machines and by now were practiced in all types of fine and fancy stitching, though Zena was a bit slower. I felt I could keep up with the best of them, though I wasn't yet entirely certain if I really wanted to go to work at a real job for the Kickernick Company and was I more or less obligated to do so? The wages I would earn there could help me get to Chicago, to be with Arnold and Violet. Still, should I give Kickernick's a try, if given the chance, perhaps through the summer and then go after saving up for the train ticket?

I had received a letter from Mrs. Powers there:

Dear Ethelyn,

I'm writing to report that your sister and brother are doing well in my home. I am happy to have them and call them my own.

As expressed by the Fairbault Home for Children, I could do with your help and would be very pleased to have you. I send my laundry out, but there is always something to do and the children need entertaining. I would hope you could cook, clean and do your best at filling in for me, as needed.

You are welcome in my home and would have an adequate room to yourself. I know you will be 17 in January, and you could be my domestic for as long as you care to stay. At Christmas, I will have a photograph made of the children and send one to you.

Kindest regards,
Mother Powers

A domestic in Chicago? I thought of these things as I whirred one piece of fabric after another into my machine. I was fast and accurate, I knew that, and, except for the dull ache behind my left shoulder at the end of each day, I liked the work.

After two weeks in the working section of the sewing room, Mrs. Kickernick came to my machine and said she already knew that Mr. Kickernick wanted me to have a position in his company come January. "I told him of your quotas and fine work. He remembers you from the baseball team."

"Thank you. I'll have to think about it," I said.

"Think about it? What is there to think about, you silly girl? Others here are killing themselves for the chance."

"It's just that...my brother and sister..."

"If you are not serious here, you can be removed from the program now, you know."

"No, I...didn't know that."

"I've said enough," Mrs. Kickernick said, and walked away.

Mrs. Kickernick moved over to Zena's machine and began talking with her. Over the sound of the machines, I couldn't catch all that was being said, but enough to understand that the teacher was telling Zena she wouldn't be admitted to the Kickernick Company. When Mrs. Kickernick left her, Zena dropped her head onto the machine and began to cry.

We were not allowed to leave our machines until the lunch bell, but I leaned over toward Zena.

"It's alright, honey. Any other company will be glad to have you. Don't forget, there's Munsingwear and I hear they're always hiring."

"It's hopeless. My mother'll kill me," Zena sobbed.

I stood to go over to Zena, but hadn't seen that Mrs. Kickernick had come up from behind me.

"Sit back down, now!" she barked at me.

She had startled me so that, as I tried to sit, my foot caught the leg of my chair. To keep from falling sideways, I quick shuffled my other foot and accidentally placed it on the foot pedal of the machine, and my hand landed just under the needle as it began to pump. The needle punctured clear through, in the space between my first and second knuckle. The machine jammed there, impaling my finger in place.

I screamed and Zena jumped up.

"Oh!" Mrs. Kickernick reached around my head for the manual wheel. She quickly brought the needle up with a hard push on it. "Look! Look what you've done!"

Blood now gushed onto the fine white cloth of a bed robe I had been hemming. I fell into the chair, my finger still on the strike plate. I was dizzy.

"Move away! Now! You're ruining the cloth!"

I slumped toward Zena, who caught me. She grabbed her own fabric and wrapped it around my finger.

We stood there shaking and looking at the blood on my machine.

"Get out! Go find the canteen manager. He has first aide." Mrs. Kickernick wiped the machine with the ruined cloth.

Zena helped me out the door.

Einar was just putting the top on his thermos at his usual table in the canteen and jumped up when he saw us.

"Dollface, what happened?"

"A needle..." I began.

"Let's get you fixed up." Einar found the canteen manager, who scrambled to get a box from under his counter.

"Give it to me," Einar barked at him.

Einar sat me down and removed the blood-soaked cloth.

"Happens all the time in Sheet Metal. I thought you girls were more careful," he said, trying to make me smile.

He placed some gauze over the still bleeding wound, then took a handkerchief from his back pocket to dry my tears.

"Zena, go tell Mrs. Kickernick Ethelyn's going home for the day and get back to work yourself. I can take her."

"It's my fault. It's all my fault," Zena cried.

"Hush now. Just go," Einar said.

He grabbed his coat from the back of a canteen chair and put it around my shoulders. He then steered me out to the street. "There's a nurse at Home School, ain't there?"

"Yes," I managed to say. My teeth were chattering now. I leaned on him for the entire streetcar ride to Home School, my head and hand pounding.

I pointed the way to the nurse's exam room in the back. When Einar reached the doorway I heard Nurse Perlich bark, "No men in here!"

She could not see that I was behind him.

"We got some blood here. Can you help?"

Nurse Perlich jumped up to take me from him and put me on the stool.

"Go now," she said to Einar. "No men, or boys, allowed here."

"I'll check on you tomorrow, honey. It's Saturday." He dashed out the door.

I just nodded, watching the nurse remove the rough bandage Einar had fashioned.

"I think the bleeding's just stopped," she said. "We'll get you over to the infirmary on Franklin. I can't be certain, but I think you may have broken a bone in there."

I had indeed broken the bone. After Dr. Vanesek had cleaned the wound, the bone protruded slightly from the palm side of my mangled finger. I got woozy looking at it.

The doctor took Nurse Perlich aside, but I heard him whisper," "It's a mess. I believe it may be best if we have the finger off."

"Off?" I moaned.

"I'm sorry, but you've damaged everything in the lower half of that finger of yours," the doctor said, moving back to me. "I'll give you ether, and you'll sleep through it and be awake in a little while. It won't take long."

I awoke in the infirmary room, the same one where I had rested exactly a year ago after my t.b. visit. Mrs. McAuliff, not Nurse Perlich, sat at my bedside now.

"There now, no pain?" Mrs. McAuliff asked.

"Tingling, kind of." I murmured.

"It'll be fine. We have something for the pain at Home School and we are free to go now. My car is outside. Nurse Perlich was called to a delivery while you slept."

The bandages now engulfed my hand and all its remaining fingers. It was a rusty orange color.

"If you don't get an infection, the doctor says you'll be healed by Christmas," Mrs. McAuliff said.

"But the sewing. How can I..?"

"You'll manage. I've already telephoned Dunwoody and Mrs.

Kickernick. She says you can return when you're ready. She called you a prized student."

I slept the entire ride home and then took to my bed. I stayed there the rest of the weekend.

At five o'clock on Saturday, Mrs. Hansen brought me a tray of food and a box of chocolates.

"A boy, Einar it was, leave for you downstairs," Mrs. Hansen said, handing me the fancy box.

CHAPTER 22

I visited Nurse Perlich's exam room in the Home School every other day to have the wound cleaned and a new bandage applied. I never could look. Nurse Perlich predicted my hand would be healed in time for Thanksgiving, some three weeks away.

I returned to sewing class a week after the accident, with my left hand still bandaged. Mrs. Kickernick gave me paperwork and quizzes to do, and she told me to read the manuals for the different Singer machines. After a time, she put me to work helping to check on the new girls at the front of the class and explaining to each how to do better.

The bandage was removed for the last time the weekend before Thanksgiving. Nurse Perlich looked over the wound at my bottom knuckle where the finger had been and pronounced it healed and perfectly formed. I could feel my missing finger try to move and was relieved to see the knuckle, at least, looked fairly normal, with a straight white scar across the bulge of the bone. I spent the rest of the day trying to do some hand-stitching, to get used to having one less finger to help hold the cloth. When I showed my scarred hand to Einar in the Dunwoody's canteen that Monday, he pronounced it perfect.

"Just tell folks the other guy looks worse," he joked.

I struggled my first day back at my machine, frequently dropping my cloth to the floor, but Mrs. Kickernick, who had become kinder since the accident for which she was partly to blame, told me to just go more slowly.

"Your hand will adjust quickly," the teacher said. "I've seen it before with our war boys over in the machine shop."

The day before Thanksgiving, Mrs. Kickernick told the class there was to be a graduation ceremony for them in December, in the canteen. Dunwoody's superintendent would present their diplomas, and we girls were to bring our families.

I looked at Zena, who made a face and said, "You can have my mother for the day."

I stuck my tongue out at her. I wondered if I could invite Mrs. Wiborg, since she was the one who had taught me to sew so well. As the girls filed out of the class at noon, I lingered behind to ask Mrs. Kickernick about this.

"Yes, dear. We have already invited Mrs. Wiborg to represent the Home School. She'd be glad to bring you to the ceremony, I'm sure."

As I turned to go, Mrs. Kickernick said, "Don't forget, Mr. Kickernick is expecting you bright and early on January the second. It's time you started earning your way in the world."

"Yes, ma'am," I said, relieved that the offer still stood despite my missing finger.

On the streetcar back to Home School I thought about sending an invitation to Pearl and Bernie. Could they come down for the ceremony on the train from Brooten? But, I put the idea out of my mind, deciding it was unlikely. It would be too expensive for them and besides, I'd heard not a word from the two of them since

I don't know when. I'll write to tell them the news, at least.

I would be officially released from the Home School exactly on my seventeenth birthday, January 6. Mrs. McAuliff had already told me that.

Working girls who had reached the age of 17 were not allowed to stay on at the Home School and a quick streetcar ride. In the warmer months I could even walk between the two and window shop along the way. However, since my new job would start January 2, they had arranged for me to move into the Women's Hotel a few days early. The hotel was on LaSalle, nearer to the Kickernick building than the Home School. The rules were strict at the Woman's Hotel, with a curfew and only supervised visits from callers allowed. I couldn't imagine a room of my own and how much I would miss my teammates here. And how was I to fill the evenings without my studies and the watchful eyes of Mrs. Hansen in the sitting room?

"You'll be safe there. Many of our girls have lived there," Mrs. McAuliff explained.

Zena said she hoped to join me there, if her mother would let her and she got a proper job.

I sat on my bed looking over my meager belongings, trying to imagine them at the Woman's Hotel. A Kickernick baseball uniform. My photograph of Mama sent to me by Aunt Hattie. The "Tin Woodman of Oz" book. A winter coat and boots. My coat for the dance. My beautiful Easter dress and those Easter shoes we all had all been given. My treasure box. It wouldn't be much of a chore to move it all to my new room at the hotel.

One more appearance before Judge Waite and I would be kicked out of Home School and so totally on my own.

Was it a mistake not to go to Chicago instead? Or to try, again, to join Pearl and Bernie at the logger's boarding house? Pearl had written me after I sent the graduation news, but never had really answered my earlier letter asking if there might be work for me in the lumber camp.

"Things are not good here, but I am well," Pearl had written on the postcard. "I hope your finger is fully recovered now. I will write again at Christmas. The weather has turned very cold."

From Mrs. Powers in Chicago I received a photograph of Violet and Arnold, the new baby, already looking fat and sitting up. Violet held him proudly on her lap in the formal portrait with the biggest possible bow in her hair. So big now. They were both dressed in clothes finer than any they could have had at Mama's house, and this just made me sad with missing them. Poor Mama.

It had been Mrs. Wiborg who had suggested, one Sunday, that I should stay in Minneapolis for now, rather than go to Chicago.

"If you learn this trade well at Kickernick's and get a good reference from Mr. Kickernick, you'll always be able to make your own way when you need to," she had said. "And there's that boy, Einar. I think he wants you nearby, doesn't he?"

She made my face blush with that.

Einar will get his diploma in December, too, and had a job lined up already through the Sheet Metal Workers Guild. He would continue to live with his father and help out in his store in the evenings. For his day job, Einar

would be what he called a "work out" man come January,
one of the men who climbed to the tops of Minneapolis's
tallest buildings, hammering on roofs and flashing.

"You know me, reckless and wild," he had said.
"And I'm mostly wild about you."

CHAPTER 23

Mrs. Wiborg was to drive me to the graduation ceremonies and arrived at Home School just as I was pinning on my hat. My bedroom door was open and Mrs. Wiborg gave a friendly knock before entering.

"This is for you," she said, handing me a small package wrapped loosely in Christmas paper.

"Oh, goodness!" I said, pulling out a pair of pure white gloves, the left hand featuring only four fingers and otherwise perfectly stitched. With a quick glance, you wouldn't even realize there was anything different about it. The gloves had three faux pearl buttons at each short cuff.

"I used to make all my daughters' gloves, long ago. It was time I tried my hand at it again," Mrs. Wiborg said.

"They are perfect," I said as I pulled them on. "Thank you. You have been so kind to me."

I moved to give her a peck on the cheek. She tried to shoo me away.

"No need to thank me, dear. You deserve it," Mrs. Wiborg said. "These should suit you well as you go out into the world. You will be missed here."

Einar joined the small gathering of sewing school graduates and their few relatives for the coffee and cake reception in Dunwoody's canteen, which was decorated in patriotic bunting for the occasion. He handed me a small bouquet of daisies as I sipped coffee with Mrs. Wiborg after the superintendent had shaken each of our hands.

"I'm proud of you, doll," he said. "Guess we'll both be joining the working classes now."

With that, Mrs. Wiborg set down her coffee cup, patted Einar's shoulder and said, "Einar, I'm trusting you to bring her home safely tonight, 10 o'clock sharp."

I looked at Einar, puzzled.

"Yep, I am to be your escort the rest of the evening," he said.

He held out his elbow to me and, as I took it, I looked to Mrs. Wiborg for her approval.

"It's fine, dear. Have a lovely stroll."

Outside at the street, Einar turned us toward Loring Park, a place the Home School girls had been taken for picnics a few times.

"We'll catch the streetcar on the other side. I know the way and it's a lovely evening, isn't it?" He held onto the hand I had crooked around his arm.

As we turned into the nearest corner of the large park, we could see skaters on the small lake, heard their laughter even from this distance.

"We'll bring our kids here, for the skating," he said as we reached the frozen lake.

"Oh, we will, will we?" I looked up at him.

"Sure. That's what I'll put my first wages to. Skates for both of us, so we learn first."

"It'll take yours and mine put together for a year," I said. "Baseball is less expensive. Let's teach them that instead."

"Deal."

CHAPTER 24

I wanted to be sure to arrive on time for my first day of work, but I hadn't realized how quickly the streetcar would get me to the Kickernick Building. It was not so far from the courthouse where I had been presented to Judge Waite last week, he signing the papers to say I was done at Home School.

Alone in another big room full of sewing machines, a matron showed me to a machine and table at the very back. She gave me a pile of child-sized slips.

"Hem these for a start. Lunch is one half-hour, at noon only. No exceptions. Don't eat over the materials. Darlene will bring more work to you later."

That was my introduction to the working world of adults. I looked around to see a dozen or so other girls coming in the front door. In the group, I noticed a girl from the Dunwoody class, one of the few who had been singled out by Mrs. Kickernick. The matron was bringing her to the machine in front of mine.

"Hello," the girl said the minute the matron had walked away. "Can you do all this with that finger of yours?"

"It's like it never happened," I whispered. "My second finger has learned what to do."

"I'm so sorry Zena didn't get chosen," the girl said.

"Me, too. But, we're roommates now. Zena's gotten on with Munsingwear."

A bell sounded and the matron shouted from the front, "Get those machines working now, please."

I worked furiously until noon, losing count of the number of slips I had hemmed. After the lunch bell rang, a man's voice came from behind my chair and said, "There's the special girl I've met before."

I turned and recognized the man who had supplied our baseball team so many months ago.

"I asked matron to sit you back here by me," he said. He gestured to the very back of the room. "That there is the boss's office. I can keep an eye on you from there."

"Thank you," was all I could think to say. "For the job, I mean."

"Oh, I love taking care of the poor girls like you. Now, don't let me keep you from your lunch," he said, and spun back toward his office. I watched him go and as he looked back at me from his office door, he winked.

At the end of my first week, the matron walked around to each girl and handed each an envelope. Inside mine I found more money than I had ever held in my hands before. From it, I would pay my second week's rent at the Women's Hotel and, I decided then and there, save to buy a proper hat.

I quickly grew used to the rhythm of my working day by the second week. Zena and I parted ways each morning from the streetcar, my stop being first, and we would find each other for dinner at the Woman's Hotel each evening, unless I lingered too long talking with Einar where he met his streetcar home. If the weather wasn't frigid cold, we walked to where he could make take a different streetcar home with him telling me about all his adventures on top of the city's buildings near and far, and we would grab a coffee before going our separate ways.

Last Thursday, on my birthday, Einar had met me with a card featuring a verse.

"This is the wish that speeds to-day,
On Love's untiring wings-
May every day that breaks anew
unfailingly come fraught to you,
with life's most treasured things."

And he had signed it, "You're my life's most treasured thing."

I kept that card tucked into my pocketbook now, to read on the streetcar.

My second weekly paycheck proved I had enough money now to buy a hat. Donaldson's was open late along with all the other stores on Fridays, and I knew Einar would be helping with his father's grocery this evening. Pushing through the Friday crowds at the brightly lit store, I felt like a proper working woman now, shopping with the same type of ladies who spent their days helping poor girls at Home School and the like. I had never had cause or money to step into the magical place and so, first thing inside, I found a postcard featuring a picture of it and decided to send it to Pearl and Bernie, to show how far I'd come up in the world.

A clerk helped me at the hat counter as I tried on several hats and finally selected the cheapest one, knowing I could make it a little prettier with some fabric I had stashed away. It was a bit large for me, though, and I knew I did not have the proper tools to adjust it correctly.

"You do alterations?" I asked the elderly clerk who had been showing me the hats. "I'd like this made a bit smaller, please."
"

Certainly, miss." The clerk banged a bell on her counter. "Miss Thompson!"

Miss Thompson? How did the clerk know my name, I wondered. My mouth dropped open when I saw who it was that came out from a curtained doorway behind the clerk. It was Pearl carrying a tall pile of fabric in her arms.

"Yes, Mrs..." she was saying to her boss.

"Pearl? Pearl!" I shouted too loudly.

"Ethelyn? What on earth..."

The clerk woman said, "Pearl here will take your instructions, miss. Pick it up next Friday."

She moved far down the counter to help another customer, giving Pearl a look as she passed by.

"Why aren't you in Brooten?" I now whispered over the counter, thinking I wanted to jump over it and give her a hug. "Where's Bernie?"

Pearl glanced over to her supervisor.

"Oh, Ethelyn, Bernie's gone off with a lumber man. It's a terrible story," she whispered. "I spent every dime to come down here looking for her."

"Looking for Bernie? What do you mean?" I was speaking too loudly again and the head clerk was heading back our way. "Where are you staying?"

"I can't tell you here," Pearl whispered, her eyes on the approaching supervisor.

I thought for a minute. There was no time to explain where I lived.

159

"Why not meet me in Loring Park on Saturday at 1 o'clock? Do you remember where it is?"

"Of course," Pearl hissed. "I'm not stupid, you know. Now go."

CHAPTER 25

I was all alone on the same Loring Park bridge where Einar and I watched the skaters back in December. I clung to the handle of the lunch bucket I had brought packed with more than the usual amount of bread and cheese, in case Pearl didn't have her own.

I saw no sign of Pearl so I passed the time by unpacking the pail and setting the food out on the bridge wall. Then I noticed her coming up the walk at the far end of the park, hunched over in nearly the same way I remembered Mama walking, all business and looking down. She wore a man's coat far too large for her and she looked terribly thin.

I gave her a quick hug around the shoulders when she reached me, but she immediately began to speak.

"Oh, Ethelyn, Bernie never did work a day once we got to Brooten. She spent her time in the dining hall, flirting with the lumberjacks instead of waitressing, and when Aunt Sigrid finally caught on, Bernie was booted out."

"Oh, dear," I said as I handed her a slice of cheese.

"Bernie told me one of the haulers knew of a good job for her, a position as a domestic in another lumber camp over to Brainerd, and he had offered to take her there. I couldn't stop her and, besides, I needed to keep my position there, not follow her and her chasing rainbows, didn't I?"

Pearl chewed the cheese and looked at me as if wanting an answer.

"No, of course not," was all I could think to say. "I mean you had to keep your job, yes."

"Pretty soon, another girl showed up in Brooten and tells us all how she had come from that Brainerd place, escaped really, when a truckload of girls was picked up from there in the middle of the night. She heard them screaming and managed to get out a back door, walked through the woods to hitch a ride once she got to Alexandria and made it to Brooten."

"Oh, dear. Where were they taking the other girls?" I asked.

"We found out later, from a church lady who came to be a missionary to us, that girls like that are taken all the time down here to Minneapolis and they...."

Pearl stopped talking and began to cry. I don't think I'd ever seen Pearl cry. Not even when Papa died, or little sister Sadie when she died on the railroad tracks in Albert Lea.

"They what, Pearl?" I prodded her to get her to continue.

"They turn them into prostitutes!"

"Oh, Pearl, really? I don't believe it. Not Bernie." I didn't realize I was madly shaking her elbow. She pulled it away from me.

"Read the papers. It's all anybody talks about these days, since the war is done. Minneapolis. St. Paul. It's all over the place."

I had not heard these stories and could have kicked myself now. So selfish and stupid. My job now and school before that. Who had time to read newspapers?

"There are gangs running brothels. Mafia. That sort of thing," Pearl continued. "Police are usually in on it somehow, and the mayor. The ladies at my mission house where I stay now make it their business to get the girls out. They do what they can, but they're just missionary ladies."

"So, you think Bernie's in one of them? How does a person find such an awful place and get them out?"

I couldn't imagine it possible. The city was so big, full of people minding their own business and looking the other way. So many here now spoke different languages, not just Norwegian.

"That's what I'm trying to learn, dammit." Pearl spun herself around to lean against the bridge wall.

"Why didn't you come find me at Home School? I can help too, you know." I knew it was not the time to get mad at Pearl, but I couldn't help it.

"I got the job the minute I got to town two weeks ago, you know, the Christmas rush at Donaldson's? I was going to come find you. Honest. But, after work I started going around to other mission houses and asking about her and getting any information I could. Somebody's always got a story to tell me and how many girls named Bernie could there be? Somebody always knows where the bad houses are. They've mentioned two or three of them on the far side of the river."

I slammed my sandwich down on the wall. "We just have to find her then. She can live with me at my hotel. I'll sneak her in until she can pay."

"Ethelyn, a lot of these girls end up dead and nobody ever knows the difference. I don't think we can just walk into one of these places and ask for Bernie. They'll lie. She'll have changed her name, or been drugged or something." Pearl began to cry again.

After a long quiet between us, she said. "I haven't been a good big sister to you, or to Bernie."

"Oh, shush," I said and moved to hug her, but she just squirmed out of the embrace. I drew back and thought a moment.

"Einar! We'll ask Einar. He hangs around with men, lots of them not such great men, in not such great neighborhoods. I bet he could find out who to ask anyway."

"Einar?"

"He's kind of my beau," I said. "He's a sheet metal worker."

Pearl smiled a little. "I always knew you'd be the one of us to make something of yourself."

"What do you mean?" I said. "It ain't like Einar's a rich man. He's just...nice, is all. But more importantly, he knows people in this city."

CHAPTER 26

I found Einar very early on Monday morning at the streetcar stop I knew he always used. He looked surprised to see me walking toward him since our morning schedules didn't usually match up.

"Dollface, you found me. Are you playing hooky from work today?"

I pulled his elbow to take him aside even though the bell was already ringing to alert everyone the streetcar was coming.

"Einar, you have to help me, me and my sisters," I said in a whisper.

"Your sisters, I thought they were all..."

"Listen now. Pearl's back in town and she says Bernie is here somewhere doing God knows what. She thinks some bad men got her involved in...in...being bad. You know."

I was too embarrassed to say it, but I think Einar understood. I'd never seen his face look so serious. He straightened up to see the streetcar coming.

"Leave it to me, doll." he said, and gave me a quick peck on the cheek. "I know a guy."

"You can't tell anybody what you're up to. We'll just die of shame."

"I know how to do this, honey. Don't worry."

The car clanged its bell again as it came up Marquette.

"I'll be in trouble if I don't grab this one, honey. Meet me Wednesday after work at the usual stop and I'll tell you what I find out."

He hopped onto the step of the streetcar before it was fully stopped and blew me a kiss as he paid his fare.

Wednesday. Two whole days to do nothing toward saving Bernie. The thought made me jumpy. I tried to calculate whether to wait for the streetcar or run to get to work on time.

"You're late," Mr. Kickernick said, though he was smiling at me as I raced to my machine by his back office.

"Sorry, Mr. Kickernick. Some problem with the streetcar," I said, removing my coat. "I'll stay later tonight."

I was so preoccupied with thoughts of Bernie that I ruined two pair of lady underdrawers first thing. I knew I couldn't risk using my short lunch break to walk over to Donaldson's and tell Pearl what Einar had said. She was going to be worried sick, I thought.

I intentionally came in early to work on Wednesday. I didn't want to be late again and, besides, my worry had me awake long before I needed to be. I had to be at Einar's streetcar stop exactly at 6 o'clock that evening to hear what he might have learned. The matron gave me fewer than the usual number of slips to work on and I raced through them, wanting to get the day done, but the slips were finished by two o'clock. I asked matron for special projects to work on, to keep my afternoon busy and I was given some fancy work for the first time. With these I could at least earn a little bonus in Friday's wage packet.

The other girls had already left their sewing machines for the day while I worked to complete the last two bed dresses from the matron. At 5:45, I was the only girl left in the big room.

"Miss Ethelyn, are you still here?"

Mr. Kickernick's loud voice from the back startled me. He was shutting down the lights to his office.

"If I can go home and I'm the boss, surely you can call it a day now?"

"Yes, sir. Just finishing up."

He was behind me at the machine before I finished speaking and he placed his hands on my shoulders.

"Mighty fine work, as always. That's why I need you," he said, leaning his chin on the top of my head. I was struck still.

"Thank you, but I guess I will go now," I said as I reached for my coat that hung on a peg next to the machine.

"They say it's started to snow out there," Mr. Kickernick said. We never could tell what was happening outside, our big sewing room had no windows.

"Perhaps I should drive you in my Ford if that's the only wrap you have?"

"Thank you. This is warm enough," I said and struggled to push my chair back without pushing into him.

"Don't be silly. It's no trouble," he said.

I turned to protest again and he quick grabbed my shoulders and kissed me hard on the mouth.

I struggled free and tried to speak, but he said, "There now. That's for my favorite girl. Let me get you a coat, it's a sample we have back in my office, and we'll be going."

I gathered my own coat and grabbed my pocketbook. Could I run for the front door before he returned? The coat got caught on the handle of my machine, trapping me as I tugged at it.

"Put this on." He was behind me again. "It's warmer than any cloth coat they make over at that old Munsingwear."

"Thank you, but I think I'd rather just ride home by myself. My fella will be waiting for me at the stop."

I was desperate to let this man know I was not alone in the world and not available to him, so old and wealthy and smelling of cigars.

"Perhaps we can pass by there, pick him up, too," he said, and he held the brown mink coat open for me to put my arms through.

I could think of no escape, but to put on the coat.

"I'm just parked out back. Have you ridden in a motor car before?"

"Yes, sir. Several times."

"Well, not like this one, you haven't. Top of the line. You're in for a treat. So much warmer than that ol' streetcar, you'll see. Not so...odorous."

I thought nothing could smell worse than this man and the cigar smell in his clothes.

Down in his car, he leaned over to my seat to show how the heating worked.

"You'll be toasty in no time," he said and, after shifting out onto Washington Avenue, he placed his arm behind me on the seat.

"Good girls like you can get ahead in the world, Ethelyn," he said, as he sped past where Einar would have been waiting for me. I craned my neck to look for his usual striped overalls, his striped cap, but I didn't see him.

I was getting too warm in the mink coat and the heat blasting in my face. It had not begun to snow. Mr. Kickernick had lied about that, it was clear.

"Turn here, at Nicollet," I said. "I'm just a few blocks down at LaSalle."

He did not turn right, but continued along Washington Avenue toward the Snoose Boulevard neighborhood I knew from Papa's drinking days.

"I know a bar. We should have a drink to warm us."

"I am not cold, Mr. Kickernick, and I must be getting home."

He looked across the seat at me.

"This time, okay. I'll let you go. My wife will be holding supper, I suspect, but I want to do this with you next Wednesday. We'll even go out to dinner. Take you to The Flame."

"I will have to see, sir. The hotel matron doesn't allow..."

"Forget her," he said, turning from the wheel to her. "I can take you places, kid."

"Please, turn here now. You can circle back to LaSalle at Portland."

He swerved hard to take the turn too fast, causing me to slide into him. "See, you want to be close to your daddy now."

"My daddy is long dead, sir." I heaved myself away from him.

I began pulling the mink coat from my shoulders as he slowed to park at my building.

"No, honey. You keep that now. I got a million more where that came from. Consider it a down-payment."

169

Not wanting to say another word to him, I got out of the door as quickly as I could.

"Night, doll. I'll be waiting for you next Wednesday, don't forget."

I slammed the door and ran up the hotel's steps.

The dining room was just emptying out but I spotted Zena reading a book at a back table.

"Thought you were meeting up with Einar tonight," Zena said when I rushed up and pulled out a chair. "Goodness, hon, where's the fire?"

I gushed out my story of the coat and kiss.

"What a creep," Zena said. "He sounds like my good old dad. I wonder if you should tell the matron what he did?"

"I'm pretty sure that would get me fired, not him," I said. "No. I'll ignore him. I'll leave work early or something, before he sees me."

I had not told Zena about Bernie and what she might be doing at this moment. I was too ashamed and there hadn't been any time.

I risked a chance at being late again the following morning and found Einar at his streetcar stop.

"Honey, what happened? I waited 'til the streetcars stopped running last night!"

"Oh, it was horrible. That ugly Mr. Kickernick insisted on driving me home last night. Now he wants a date-a date!-with me next Wednesday."

I was shaking, still angry at the memory of last night's trip home.

"Kickernick is what I was going to tell you last night," Einar said, moving the two of them under an awning to get out of the light snow.

"What? What about him?"

"He's a ringleader for a gang that runs most of the cat houses in this city."

"What?" I moved away to see his face. "Who told you this?"

"A cop. He walks the beat near us guys at the other end of Franklin where we've been working on the bridge. He's a good cop."

"But if a policeman knows of the bad things going on, why doesn't he have Kickernick arrested?'

"He says they're working on it, but they need to know where the houses are, exactly. Our detectives are on it, too. They got hunches, but they need to catch somebody in the act," Einar said. "Every Wednesday, Kickernick rounds up his gang at The Flame and the cops are on to him there."

"I don't understand. And where's Bernie? I just want to find her is all."

"If the coppers can get to the houses, they might find her and...wait a minute."

Einar pulled his cap off and I could see he was thinking.

"What? They might find her and...what?" I looked up at him.

"Maybe you can be helpful to the cops?"

"What? Me? What do you mean?"

"Let Kickernick take you where he wants to go on Wednesday. Maybe our cop can follow you? Yeah."

"Oh, don't be ridiculous. I don't want to go with Kickernick. That creep."

"But it could be our chance to find Bernie," Einar said, pulling me to him.

"What, next Wednesday?"

"Only if you and I can meet before then, say Saturday. Can we meet in Loring, after our shifts?"

I agreed, not really thinking he was that serious, but I told him I'd also see about having Pearl meet us, too. "She's been doing a little of her own detective work," I said. "And she's got to know what we're planning."

I was late into work again that morning.

"Don't forget we got a date next week, doll," Mr. Kickernick greeted her at the door. "I'll have a new hat for you, to go with the coat, so wear the coat."

"I have a hat, thank you," I said, though her plan was to see Pearl on Friday at Donaldson's on the pretext of picking up her new, altered hat.

"Oh, well, aren't you the rich girl now that I'm paying you?" Kickernick said. "Don't forget that. Wednesday."

I was relieved to see the matron heading his way so he had to stop talking to me.

At Donaldson's Friday night, the clerk recognized me and immediately summoned Pearl from the back room.

"The lady's hat please, Miss Thompson." Pearl gave me a professional nod and retreated to her room at the back.

"Here you are," Pearl said to me like I was just another customer. "You'll want to try it on."

"Einar will help us," I whispered as soon as the clerk had moved away. "He's talking to his friends. Can you meet us at Loring Park tomorrow?"

"Yes, I guess so," Pearl whispered. "At one o'clock."

CHAPTER 27

On the Loring Park bridge on Saturday, Einar told me and Pearl what he found out. The cop he knew had gotten to the detectives and they had quickly put together a plan.

He said I could go with Mr. Kickernick next Wednesday, as he was expecting, and the police would be waiting on the street, parked near his Kickernick building.

"They have been watching him a long time and his business, and they know the first stop where he takes the girls-The Flame Restaurant."

I gasped. "That's where he said he's taking me."

Einar said. "Here's my guy now."

I followed Einar's gaze down the sidewalk, where a man wearing a dark coat approached them.

"He's our copper," Einar whispered in my ear.

The man tipped his hat as he came up. "Miss," he said to Pearl, then me.

"You're the one works for Kickernick?" the man asked me.

"Yes, sir."

"Thought so. I've seen you come out of his building. We're watching that place," the man said. "You learn sewing at Dunwoody?"

"Yes, how did you know?"

"Kickernick's got this whole thing rigged real nice, preying on the Dunwoody gals where his wife works," the cop said. "Look, we know Kickernick always hands over his girls to a big guy, they call him Red Hat, a guy we've had our eyes on for a long time."

"Kickernick takes you to The Flame over in Snoose, see, and we follow. You'll meet Red Hat, probably. Kickernick likes to keep his hands clean. We'll tail you from the Flame to wherever. Then we nab the madam of the house and maybe we find your sister. We'll find lots of girls, that's for sure, if not your sister. Will you help us?"

I looked up to Einar, who turned to address the cop.

"You're double sure you can follow this Red Hat guy wherever he takes Ethelyn?"

"It's what we do all the time. She'll be safe, I promise," the man said. "We'll be right behind and she'll be doing this city a good turn."

"That sounds too dangerous, Ethelyn. You can't do it," Pearl said. "I won't allow you to."

"I will so do it," I said. Einar put his arms around me. I looked up at him and said, "I'm not scared."

CHAPTER 28

To sit through two more days of working was sheer torture, with Mr. Kickernick winking at me each time he passed my machine.

After meeting with Einar and the cop, I thought I might go mad if I didn't tell someone about this crazy plan, wondering if I was crazy myself to even consider being part of it. I told Zena that night while the others listened to music in the sitting parlor at the Woman's Hotel. I was hoping the music would drown out my Bernie story.

"I don't believe it!" was Zena's response. "You mean my lousy mother was right about white slavery?"

"I don't know about that, but I know what's happened to Bernie," I said. "Zena, I'm so scared. Next Wednesday, will you watch for me and try to make up some excuse why I'm not there when the bell rings for bed?"

"Love to, doll. It's the least I can do," Zena said. "Oh, it's so exciting. I wonder if you'll be in the papers."

"God, I hope not."

I boarded the streetcar on the morning of my "date" with Kickernick, feeling ridiculous in the mink coat he had told me to wear. These people who saw me every morning, who I have chatted with, were going to think I sold myself out to some rich man. I was sure of it.

When the bell rang at the end of the workday, I waited for all the others to leave, pretending to be too engrossed in my work to stop. Mr. Kickernick didn't waste any time. He was behind me the second the matron left, as if he had been waiting for just that thing before coming out of his office.

"It's you and me, baby," he said over my head.

"Yes, sir. Let me put on my coat."

"I've got that. You've got to get used to a man taking care of you now."

"Yes sir," I mumbled.

As we pulled out onto Washington Avenue, I tried to imagine where the men in the police car were among the few ordinary cars at the sidewalk. The cars and people all looked the same to me, nobody paying any attention to the two of us.

"Don't be nervous, doll. You ever had a drink before?"

"Yes, sir, plenty of times," I said, though one swallow of something Einar had brought to the dance last October probably didn't count.

"Oh, see. I knew you had it in you," he said and tried to pull me closer to him.

The building he pulled up to was brightly lit on the street side, with a lit up sign that said "The Flame" next to the door. I'd been in this neighborhood with Papa, at some time in that other life. Mr. Kickernick pulled around the corner and drove into an alley behind the building. He knocked on an unmarked door with a single dim red bulb shining above it.

Inside was total darkness except for some gas lamps flickering feebly in the far corners. A little stage was at the far end, but Mr. Kickernick maneuvered me toward the bar where a man stood drying glasses with a towel.

"Jake, this here's my girl for the night. You take care of the two of us now, you hear. We'll have the usual."

"Yes, Mr. Kickernick. Coming up," the man said in a heavy accent.

We sat in a semi-circular booth to the right of the stage and there was no one else in the place except three big men playing cards at another table. I immediately noticed the biggest one was wearing the red hat the cops said he would. My heart leapt into my throat.

"Drink up, honey!" Mr. Kickernick said as the bartender set drinks in front of us. Kickernick's was a tankard of beer and mine was in a tall, delicate glass with a long stem.

"This here's a martini. I bet you haven't had one of those?" he said, handing me the glass.

"No, sir." I eyed the drink.

"Cheers now," he said and tipped the stem towards my mouth as he drank with his other hand. "To us."

I waited for him to drink, nearly half the tankard it turned out, as I tried to take the tiniest sip of the clear liquid in my own glass.

"Come on. It won't bite." He tilted the glass toward my mouth again and chuckled. "Actually it kind of does until you get used to it, don't it?"

I took another of the smallest sips possible and gasped a little even at that.

"See, I told you? Good though, huh?"

Just then a curtain opened on the stage, music began playing, and a young, olive-skinned woman with very black hair came out clicking something in her hands and stomping her feet on the wooden floor.

"Ah, Consuelo tonight. She's good." Mr. Kickernick watched the dancing woman.

I took another sip of the horrid drink before Mr. Kickernick could goad me into it.

I tried to keep up with the twirling moves the woman was making, but it made me dizzy. I looked away and the table seemed to be moving under my drink. Before my thoughts could clear, Consuelo finished her act and left the stage. Mr. Kickernick snapped his finger toward the group of men at the other table.

"Doll, I gotta go put in an appearance with the missus, but I want to meet you later. I've got a little place by one of the lakes, beautiful scenery. This gentleman here will take you there and you wait for me. We'll dance. Have a nice dinner."

I tried to look up at the huge man now standing at our their table, but I couldn't focus on his eyes. His red hat was a big, blurry smudge.

"No...I...want...to...go...home." I couldn't get the words in my head out my mouth.

"Red Hat here will take you home then. He'll take care of you. You just tell him where, honey."

I needed to steady myself on the table when I stood up. The big man grabbed me under the arms and helped me upright.

"See you later, doll," Mr. Kickernick called after us.

The big man led me out the same back door we had come in, where a lorry was now parked with its back door propped open. All I could think of was the poor Binders, the Germans who had died of the flu in our neighborhood. Was that yesterday, I thought?

"No, I don't want to die," I heard myself screaming as Red Hat picked me up and shoved me into the back of the vehicle.

"Nobody's dying, sweetheart. Now get in and take a nice nap. We'll be there in no time."

He pushed me once more and slammed the door on me. I could feel the lorry start to move, which made a nice movement that rocked me to sleep.

My legs were so cold, so cold. I sat up to grab a blanket and realized where I was, the lorry was stopped now, its door open. How long had I been asleep? Then I saw Red Hat reaching in to grab one of my legs and I kicked at him.

"Stop there, you!" I heard a booming voice somewhere behind Red Hat. "You'll be taking only us in with you this time. Leave the girl."

Red Hat was yanked back from the lorry door by three uniformed police officers. They struggled to turn him around and as they did, I could see one of them had shoved a pistol into Red Hat's back.

They are police. It's okay, it's okay, I told myself. The cold air cleared my head. I sat up to watch the policemen shove Red Hat toward a dimly lit cellar door just to the left. Red Hat knocked on the door twice, waited, then knocked three more times. I waited until I saw they had all gone through the cellar door, then I scrambled out to follow.

I crouched to the side of the open door and in seconds heard girls screaming and an older woman's voice say, "Now wait a minute."

Red Hat swore at the police. One of the three officers put handcuffs on a woman who was trying to bar the entryway, while two others struggled with Red Hat and got handcufffs on him.

Red Hat and the woman were led out the door and to the lorry I had just escaped. They were shoved inside and one cop slammed a crow bar between the handles. He turned and saw me where I crouched.

"Young lady, you're not to go in there," he said, motioning to the cellar door and he ran in.

But I sprang up and jostled passed the two other officers inside. They paid no attention to me and were opening tiny doors on each side of a long, dim hallway. Each room had a girl in it, sitting on the far corner of a flimsy bed. One had a girl and an old man, both of them mostly not dressed. An officer barged into this room and grabbed the man by the neck, tossing him out to another cop. I followed the last officer as he opened more doors. I stood behind him covering my ears as he kicked in the last door. I immediately recognized Bernie, though heavy make-up smudged her eyes.

"Bernie!" I pushed the officer out of my way. "Bernie!"

"Who the hell...Gerty? That you?" Bernie said.

"We've got to get you out of here. Pearl is so worried."

"Pearl? She's in Brooten, that rat hole of a place she took me to."

Bernie sounded like she was half asleep still.

"No," I said. "She's here, looking for you."

"Where's here?" Bernie asked.

"Minneapolis, don't you know that?" I shook her a little bit, but then the cop pulled me away.

"Come on girls, this ain't a hen party," he said. "Your sister's got to come with us, lady, but you can get yourself to the precinct in the morning, bail her out."

I hung onto Bernie's shoulders as the cop led her outside, the three of us barely fitting through the narrow hallway. As the officer loaded Bernie into another lorry, this one with a "Minneapolis Police" star on its door, I saw Mr. Kickernick was already inside, smiling at me from the bench, his hands in front of him in handcuffs.

"You!" I yelled.

I bent and grabbed at my own boot, took it off and flung it at Kickernick, hitting him squarely on the forehead.

"Keep the coat, doll. But, you're fired."

CHAPTER 29

I had to shoo Violet and Arnold off my lap as Mrs. Powers handed me the coffee in a fine china cup.

"Go now, we can play more later," I told the children.

"Thank you, Mrs. Powers." I watched Violet climb onto Einar's lap across the parlor.

"Wiggle, wiggle," Violet was saying to Einar, touching his ears.

We only just arrived that morning, but Einar had already demonstrated his magical ears for everyone. Arnold toddled around us, laughing simply because we were laughing.

"You were so good to let us come," I said to Mrs. Powers, a primly dressed, thin woman who reminded me of a younger Mrs. McAuliff. "I just couldn't believe it when Einar handed me our train tickets."

"A honeymoon in Chicago," the woman sang. "I'm not sure how romantic that is, but the two of you appear to be happy?"

"We're the best," I answered, "Though it's also been a sad time with Einar's father dying this spring. Einar inherited a little, so he had this idea we get married as soon as respectable after."

What a whirlwind of sadness and happiness it had been, I thought. And now to be reunited with Violet and to meet Arthur, I realized how little time I'd had to think about Mama and Papa and their own deaths. I missed them more today than I had all together in the nearly three years since the flu epidemic had scattered us all to the winds, landing us in the new lives we all lived now. Who could have imagined?

Though I had only just met Mr. Bertelsen, Einar's father, I had cried more than anybody had standing at his casket. I knew I was crying for Mama and Papa, whose funerals had been lost to me. I longed to see them one last time, even if in their own caskets. I cried for their vanished lives, gone as if erased like the teacher wiping a blackboard clean at the end of the school day. How near my sisters had come to being erased, too.

Einar didn't want to run his father's store, though it was now legally his.

"All my fancy training up on the roofs of Minneapolis? I don't want that to go to waste," he had said to me shortly after the funeral.

Who was it who had first suggested Pearl and Bernie become the shopkeepers? I couldn't say for sure now.

"Bernie had worked at Josie's store for so many years, you know. That's the one that was right in our neighborhood," I explained to Mrs. Powers. "And Pearl, well, Pearl loves bossing people around, so she seems suited to being a shopkeeper with Bernie as her employee. Plus, she's good at bookkeeping and the like, did that for Aunt Sigrid at the logging camp."

"And you?" Mrs. Powers said. "What will you do now? The outfit you brought for baby Arnold is so handsome. I can't believe you sewed it yourself."

"I'm to be a housewife, Einar says, and a mother when the times comes," I said, feeling the familiar blush on my cheeks. "Maybe I'll make a few things to sell in the Bertelsen Store to earn a few pennies."